TOMMY RED

Tommy Dalton's ex-wife is on an honesty kick with their daughter, Alysha. She tells her that her dad kills people. Which, of course, he does. But that's not the kind of information he wants shared with his kids. Particularly now that he's working on a new job. Dominick Farase, ready to testify against the Cirelli family, needs silencing. An ex-cop spots him and lets Gasper Cirelli know where to find him. Not a difficult job for Tommy Red. But the Cirellis get nervous about this one, and decide to remove all evidence of the hit—including Tommy.

More hits are called, and some of them get sloppy. A couple of FBI agents get involved. Frank Cirelli, Gasper's son and acting head of the family, has to make some tough decisions. Sacrifices must be made. But as far as Tommy is concerned, the Cirellis make their biggest mistake when they fail in their efforts to take him out. A fatal mistake. Now he's after the family—still trying to keep his daughter out of it, too, of course—because when you threaten Tommy or *his* family, the only response is retribution.

Charlie Stella Bibliography

Eddie's World (December, 2001, Carroll & Graf)

Jimmy Bench-Press (December, 2002, Carroll & Graf)

Charlie Opera (December, 2003, Carroll & Graf)

Cheapskates (March, 2005, Carroll & Graf)

Shakedown (June, 2006, Pegasus)

Mafiya (January, 2008, Pegasus)

Johnny Porno (April, 2010, Stark House)

Rough Riders (July, 2012, Stark House)

Dogfella: How an Abandoned Dog Named Bruno
Turned This Mobster's Life Around–A Memoir
(May, 2015, Da Capo Lifelong Books)

TOMMY RED
by Charlie Stella

STARK
HOUSE

Stark House Press • Eureka California

TOMMY RED

Published by Stark House Press
1315 H Street
Eureka, CA 95501
griffinskye3@sbcglobal.net
www.starkhousepress.com

TOMMY RED

ISBN: 1-933586-96-6
ISBN-13: 978-1-933586-96-0

Book design by Mark Shepard, shepgraphics.com
Director, Author Rights Agency: Svetlana Pironko

First Stark House Press Edition: April 2016

FIRST EDITION

TOMMY RED
by Charlie Stella

Dedication

We grew up around the block from one another. The first time we met, he was riding his younger brother, Michael, on a bicycle and we exchanged looks, after which he said, "What are you lookin' at?" We were 10 or 11 or so, and he had a beard so I headed straight up the stairs into our house.

Tommy was a terrific athlete, husband, father, brother and son. We went to Catholic school together, and later to the same high school. We weren't exactly studious, but we had a hell of a good time getting into trouble and playing sports. We were pretty good at coordinating lies about tests we had and failed.

In fact, our roles were pretty interchangeable when it came to subverting our parents' knowledge of how we might be doing in school.

"Charlie/Tommy, make sure you don't tell your parents about the math test today in case our fathers run into one another working the bingo tonight."

And the response would always go something like this: *"Tommy/Charlie, are you kidding? I got a 40 on that thing. What test?"*

We often used the old trolley path between our blocks (95th and 96th Streets, between Avenues M & N in Canarsie) as a baseball field with home run fences that were actually fences to safeguard vegetable gardens.

Tommy really was sprouting a beard at a very young age (probably later than when he was 10 or 11, but way before high school). Our high school football team nicknamed him "Wolfman."

We didn't see much of each other the next few years, and as chance sometimes happens, we were married on the same day, October 23, 1977. Tommy married a second cousin of mine, Linda Maita. Tommy and Linda's first born is named Nicole. My first born is also named Nicole.

There was a big gap in years between our seeing each other again. I know I was living in Manhattan, literally across the street from where I'd heard from my mother that Tommy was at NYU having a brain tumor removed. I went to visit him there. The next time we saw each other, I grabbed a couple of tickets to a Colts-Bills game up in Buffalo and we flew up there. Tommy was always a Colts (Johnny Unitas), Lakers (Jerry West) and Dodgers fan, but I forget who his favorite Dodger may have been.

Tommy was struck down by a brain tumor way too young. Nobody ever had a bad thing to say about him. He was a great guy. He is missed.

This one's for Tommy Mistretta.

And for our beloved Rigoletto.

Acknowledgement

No Stella crime novel or anything else published with my name attached could ever have happened without the help and guidance of my original writing mentor, Dave Gresham. He put up with my neophyte efforts, many of which would've driven most to drink.

Then again, he did disappear from time to time on a sailboat ....

I can never thank Dave enough. Never underestimate the power of teachers. Dave's influence was essential to my education as a writer and a thinking being. He's simply the smartest guy I've ever known. His brilliance in and out of the classroom made me want to do something I'd ignored for 18 years – my education. It was the first time in my life I took both school and reading seriously, and low and behold, the world became so much bigger than it had ever been before.

A terrific author, teacher and editor, Merle Drown, did the heavy lifting (editing) on *Tommy Red*. He's one hell of a guy, editor and author, so I don't mind repeating myself.

I also have to thank a few people for giving first reads of *Tommy Red*, some early in the drafts, and a few with a final set of revisions. Gavin Borden, Nicole Hope Caliendo, Bill Beneducci, and last but not least, the person most responsible for my staying in the writing game, the person most responsible for me never spending more than an overnight in lock-ups, my wife, my Principessa, Ann Marie.

PART I

Staten Island Ferry, New York

"I thought you was retired," Gasper Cirelli said to Quinlan King.

"I thought you were in jail," King said.

King had just sat across from Cirelli in the last row of bench seats on the top deck on the Staten Island Ferry, *Guy Molinari*. Both men in their early sixties, they sported small pot bellies and gray hair. Cirelli wore prescription sunglasses and was dressed in New York Jets sportswear: cap, jacket and sweatpants. King wore a black warm-up suit with gold piping.

"I'm retired myself now," Cirelli said. He fingered a thin gold chain with a St. Christopher metal. "Out three months. How'd you find me?"

"I'm retired doesn't mean I don't read the papers," King said. "I keep abreast of things. Saw where it was mentioned you were taking early boat rides to the city every morning. I was here at seven, didn't see you or your muscle. I finally spotted you just in time to make the seven-fifteen. One article claims you sit in different spots on the ferry every day in case somebody is trying to record your conversations. I think the guy wrote the article was being cynical after your retirement from the life and all, but that guy is usually pretty accurate. Anyway, I took a shot, got to the ferry early today."

"Gives me something to do," Cirelli said. "I feed the pigeons on the other side, Battery Park, take a walk up to the subway, take the train to Spring Street and visit the old neighborhood. Sometimes I have lunch the old place, then catch a ride home from one of the waiters lives here on the island. I pay the tolls, so he drops me off."

King smiled. The game they were playing went back some fifteen years when he was with the Organized Crime Unit assigned to the Cirelli crime family. Gasper was the eldest brother and running things until a series of cooperating witnesses involved with the Dock Workers Union brought him down. King had been one of the detectives with the task force sent to arrest Cirelli that day.

"You're an old fella enjoying his later years," King said. "I get it."

"And you?" Cirelli said. "What gets you up so early? Looking to write a book?"

"I wish. Be a good one, though, no? The shit from the old days."

"You'd need cooperation for a book. I've gone this far. I think you're out of luck."

"Nah, it's nothing like that, a book. Maybe a bit of nostalgia, though. Like I said, the article mentioned you were usually on an early ferry, so I thought I'd say hello."

Cirelli rubbed his hands together before pointing to a brown paper bag on the bench alongside him. "I have to sneak the bread from the house or my wife'll give me shit. Sometimes I buy stale bagels from the carts on the other side, break those up for the pigeons."

"You don't have to tell me about wives giving you shit," King said. "Mine's up some island in New Hampshire this week. Got a bug up her ass about a year ago, started doing arts and crafts. Painting, cutouts, laminating, frames. She saw some ad on the internet for decoupage, whatever the fuck that is. Wound up joining some class, has this shit she makes all over the house now. I told her I was gonna set it on fire she didn't move it down the basement. Now the basement is loaded with this bullshit she makes. Her class takes this annual trip, that island, they soak morons like my wife for a couple grand so they can learn to make the same shit I seen kids make in kindergarten, what it comes down to, you ask me. Decoupage."

King grabbed his crotch. "Deco this."

Cirelli smiled.

"Me, I wanna head down to Florida already, get some sun, watch the broads onna beaches there," King said. "The bathing suits today, you can see everything without having to take them off." He pointed to Cirelli's sunglasses. "Wear a pair of those and nobody's the wiser, what I'm looking at."

"I had my fill of the sun," Cirelli said. "Did my last five years in Talladega, Alabama. You can have the heat. I like the seasons, all four of them."

The ferry jerked into motion. Both men turned and looked out the window.

"The other thing about this island," King said, facing Cirelli again, "they can only shower three times a week. Imagine? A bunch of whack job broads getting up there in age are gonna work with their hands all day, go for walks, hikes, whatever, then they're gonna eat, do this, do that, and then wait every other day to clean themselves? No thank you. I told her make sure you shower before I pick you up. It's a five, six hour drive, and I don't like the wind in my ear."

"And you felt this sudden need to share this with me why?" Cirelli said.

"Like I said, I read the papers," King said.

"Yeah, to stay in touch, you said."

"More or less. It's not so much I'm nosey. I got nothin' better to do."

"You're bored."

"More or less. The thing of it is, I walked into a guy on this island I'm thinking shouldn't be breathing, much less walking around like any other citizen."

Cirelli's brow furrowed as he rubbed his hands again.

"I don't expect you're gonna take my word for it, my being a former cop and all, you're just out and happy to be so, but we can also go the bathroom, you want me to strip down, make sure I'm not wired. Or I can meet you on Mulberry Street for lunch later, you can frisk me there."

King stopped talking when a thick man with broad shoulders stood at the end of their row of seats. Cirelli waved him away and King resumed his conversation.

"I see posters of the latest reality show, *Mob Tails*, whatever the fuck. They're plastered all over the ferry terminal on my way in this morning. *Mafia Princesses.*"

"The world is upside down," Cirelli said.

"I'll say," King said. "Between that garbage, bosses flipping, the mockery being made of your thing today? Hell, it even insults me."

Cirelli yawned into a fist. "Excuse," he said.

"I know it'll never be what it was, but right now it's an aberration, your thing," King said. "*La Cosa Nostra* has become *La Cosa* freak show. I'm thinking a guy was in the protection program for taking down a heavyweight, he turned up with two behind his ear for the world to see, he gets the same level of publicity as these crazy broads doing the reality shit. It'd send a message anybody thinking of cutting a deal."

Cirelli chuckled. "A guy is gonna flip, you really think he's gonna care one out of hundred other guys made a deal winds up dead? Uncle Sam's way ahead on that scorecard, my friend. It's no secret we lost that war."

"Yeah, but maybe the guys he's about to give up care," King said, "at least a couple of skippers he worked for, which means whoever else he was involved with. The dominoes fall a lot faster and harder once somebody gets enough of a push. This guy I seen the island there, he's not inna cell for a good reason. They're hiding him, make no mistake. You know as well as I, once he testifies, there'll be a train more to follow. Like you said, it's a lost war. Problem is your side is still taking casualties.

"Besides the fact it can't hurt. The way it is now? Wiseguys, I mean. The doorbell rings, they see the badges through the peephole, start negotiating through the door."

"And what, this is some act of charity you're looking to perform?"

King shook his head. "Like I said, I'm retired. And the wife is about making me nuts with her decoupage and every other fucking thing. The day I drop her off, this island I'm talking about, New Hampshire, there's some class going on. College kids, I guess. One of the instructors there goes off every once in a while, raises his arm and yells 'Arrr!' like he's a pirate or some shit. Or maybe someone lit his balls with a blow torch, he yelled loud enough. He was standing behind me one time he did it, I nearly shit myself."

Cirelli yawned again.

"No, to answer your question," King said. "I was never big on charity, tell you the truth."

One side of Cirelli's mouth twitched. "I have to guess much longer or what?"

"Let's put it this way," King said. "I'm thinking becoming an entrepreneur my old age." He held up a finger. "The other thing, we don't have kids, me and the wife, so there's nothing keeping us together but a fading sense of obligation. It's not like she puts out anymore, and frankly I'm not interested she did. Personally, I'd like to make a move down south and leave her behind. Retire in one of them communities where you want a blow job from a broad with teeth, you call an escort service. She's also retired, the wife. It's not like she'd be hurting for cash if I disappeared. And even when she had teeth, blowjobs were always a no-no. The problem with marrying Catholic school girls were actually virgins you first plugged them."

Cirelli's smirk became a scowl. He was old school. Men weren't supposed to air their dirty laundry, especially about their wives.

"If you're trying to make me comfortable, you're doing a shitty job," he said.

"I meant no disrespect," King said.

"You need to tell that to your wife."

"Fair enough. About this other thing, this person walking around like some taxpaying citizen, is there any interest? I realize that's too vague a description for you to make onna' spot, but I have a picture or two. Maybe I can join you later the day, for lunch or whatnot. You can take a look-see."

"As a retired businessman, I have zero interest in anything to do with missing persons, what I assume you're referring to. I'll also assume you know the restaurant I frequent for lunch. In case you don't, it's on McDougal between Hester and Canal, got the quarter moon underneath the name."

"I know the place," King said. "I'm not mistaking, it's far enough away from all the protests going on, I can get there without a detour."

"Speaking of which, that's some mess your people made," Cirelli said. "Arrest a guy for hawking cigarette lighters? The fuck was that about?"

"Young and stupid, the kids did it."

"They're lucky it's Staten Island. DA won't touch them."

"They're luckier it's not Chicago. Be a bounty on their heads."

"That'll be next, the way things are today."

King nodded. "Pro'bly," he said, then shrugged. "So, I'll stop by later for lunch."

"I like the rigatoni in a Bolognese sauce," Cirelli said, "but the pasta primavera is also very good. Depends you like meat or not."

King nodded twice, stood, then headed toward the stairway for the deck below. Cirelli opened a *Staten Island Advance* and began reading about the protests against police brutality scheduled for Times Square later in the day.

■ ■ ■

Brooklyn, New York

Quinlan King was doing his retirement math for the third time since he'd eaten dinner. The pastrami on rye he'd picked up from Katz deli before he left Manhattan was upsetting his stomach. He belched into a loose fist before scratching out the last set of available cash totals. He added the figures again, this time circling the last number, two hundred thousand dollars. He underlined the same number several times before setting the pencil down.

His eyes were almost as tired as his body. It had been a busy day. He'd been on his feet more than usual. A quick guess at the miles he'd logged walking the streets of Little Italy put the number way too close to five for it not to hurt. He leaned forward on the couch to rub the bottoms of his feet when his cell phone rang for the third time since dinner.

"Fuck me," he said, then ignored his wife's call again.

Earlier in the day he'd pitched the sale of a key figure in the witness protection program to the Cirelli crime family. Dominick Farese, a soldier with the same crew, was scheduled to testify against two high ranking Cirelli captains. Farese had already served six years of an eight year manslaughter charge when federal agents played a tape of a Cirelli capo discussing how the crime family had decided to give Farese up on a second murder, sacrificing him to save the capo's son. Within minutes of hearing the tape Farese agreed to join the witness protection program and testify against the crime family he'd taken a blood oath to never betray. What King didn't know about Dominick Farese, and probably why the acting boss of the crime family, Frank Cirelli, was willing to pay for the information, was the connection between Farese and Frank's younger brother, Paul—both had taken their oaths of *omerta* on the same day some ten years ago.

Farese was thirty-three when he began serving time. The other day on the island, except for the curly hair perm, King thought Farese looked pretty much the same. The missing tip of his left pinky finger was what first caught King's attention. Farese was holding something in his left hand while reading. The missing fingertip was unavoidable. It was why King eventually took a few pictures of him.

Other distinguishing marks might've included three tattoos Farese sported: a Betty Boop on his left biceps, a cross on his right biceps, and the three letter giveaway on the small of his back—LCN. All three tattoos were done before his twenty-fifth birthday, when Farese was still young and dumb enough to mark himself. King assumed all three tattoos would have been removed by now, but that missing fingertip was more than enough to identify the wiseguy. His build and his cold stare, what King felt when Farese must've realized he was being watched and turned toward King, were good enough for a positive identification.

King was only on the island through lunch and wasn't able to learn Farese's government issued name. He did manage to learn that the former Cirelli crime family soldier was working on the conservationist island. It was more than enough information. Either the Cirellis were interested or they weren't. King would know come the morning.

In the meantime, he liked thinking about the money. It would leave him with an extra two hundred thousand dollars to live out his life, more than enough to live in comfort. He'd have to split all other assets with his wife, including his pension, but the peace of mind he'd have was more than worth it.

He returned to the pictures of Dominick Farese he'd found on Google the night before. The one with the missing fingertip stood out: Farese, his boss and his boss's son, all three holding hotdogs in front of Nathan's Famous in Coney Island, Farese's missing fingertip in full view. The caption listed the names. Dominick Farese was standing alongside "Wild" Bill La-Bella and his son, Junior. Wild Bill was the capo whose voice was recorded trying to sell Farese out for a murder that would leave him in jail the rest of his life. Wild Bill was pictured with his mouth wide open, about to take a bite from a hot dog.

King stared at the picture of the three wiseguys, then clicked onto his desktop and the link to his favorite website, the Victoria's Secret swimwear page. He took his time slowly scrolling through the pictures of bikini clad bodies. When he was bored with the swimwear, King switched to the lingerie pages. He especially liked pages with women modeling garter belts. He closed his eyes and imagined one of the blondes on the page modeling a red bustier with matching garter belts. He was excited when his cell phone rang again and ruined the moment.

"God damn it," he said.

He grabbed the cell phone and answered the call while heading to the kitchen.

"Yeah," he said.

"Quinlan, where have you been?" his wife said.

"Fuck," King mouthed. "OTB," he said.

"I've been trying to get you all night."

"I had my phone off."

"Why? You knew I'd be calling."

King rolled his eyes. "Duh," he said, turning his mouth away from the phone.

"Quinlan?"

"What?"

"Why didn't you pick up? Why'd you turn off your phone?"

"I forgot it was off is all," he said. "How's it going up there?"

"It's fine, except for the showers. I don't get to take one until tomorrow. But the class was wonderful this morning. I'm already working on my final project. The instructor said I have natural talent."

Yeah, for ball breaking, King thought.

"That's great," he said with no emotion. "How's the grub?"

"It's not too bad," his wife said. "All you can eat, but one plate is usually more than enough."

"Meet any men you want to bed down?"

"Oh, stop it. There are plenty, though, if I was that way."

"Except they're probably all fags."

"You're a Neanderthal."

"That's me."

"I have classes through noon tomorrow, but then I'm going sailing with one of the other women here who knows how. I'm not sure I'll have reception on the water, so I probably won't call until before or after dinner tomorrow. Please keep your phone on."

Feel free to drown while you're out there, King was mouthing away from the phone. "I'll have it on," he told his wife.

"Make sure, please. I don't like having to call back a thousand times a night."

"You mean two thousand."

"What?"

"Nothing. Don't worry, I'll leave my phone on."

"And don't forget to water the plants."

"I won't."

"Make sure."

"Fuck yourself," he mouthed. "I will," he said.

"Okay, then. Good night."

"Right. Good night."

"See you—"

King killed the call, turned off his phone, then returned to the Victoria Secret page. He remembered the plants and looked at them across the room.

"Yeah, right," he said. "I'll shoot myself first."

Atlantic City, New Jersey

"He says to him, he says, 'I wouldn't send a knight out on a dog like this,'" Tommy Red Dalton said. He looked at his daughter, gave it a moment, and then smiled. "Get it?"

Alysha Dalton didn't smile. Instead she said, "Mom said you're a killer. A contract killer."

Someone playing a nearby slot machine hit the progressive jackpot. The machine's bells were loud until the screaming drowned out the electronic noise. Tommy and his daughter were having drinks at a bar in the center of the casino. Tommy turned toward the noise, frowned, and ran a hand through his thick red hair.

"Dad?" Alysha said, loud this time.

Tommy leaned forward. "What?" he said, also speaking louder then. "How'm I supposed to answer something like that? Your mother said. You gonna believe me, what I say?"

"Are you or not?"

A large crowd was gathering around the newest millionaire. Someone yelled, "Holy shit!"

"You went to prison," Alysha said. "I know that much."

"Twice, in case you didn't know about the first time," Tommy said. "I was a kid the first time. Did eight months of a fifteen month bid at the BCDC for robbing a grocery store with some numbnuts I was hanging around, except I was the dumbski caught, not them. The one you do know about, the one I never hid from, was a bank job. My return to Baltimore City Detention Center. I was there for five of the eight year bid. I was the driver, by the way. I wasn't waving a gun in anybody's face, and I didn't have one on me when I was arrested. Once I was out the joint, I worked hauling soda the warehouse six blocks from where I lived. I didn't live where you lived because two years before I come out, your mother shows up the prison there, she says to me, she says, she don't love me no more, she met somebody. I didn't ask who, when, what or why. Shit like that, it happens. A guy is away, it's the price he pays. I says to her, I says, you want out, I won't get in the way. So long's you stay in Baltimore or near enough I can see my kids, you and your sisters. I says to her, you bring the guy home, make sure he don't get stupid with my girls or I'll kill him. Maybe that's what she was talking about, your mother. I threatened to kill anyone got stupid with you or your sisters, and that I would do. Kill, I mean. Somebody touched you or your sisters, I'd kill them in a heartbeat, no questions asked, but I never killed anyone my life. That's the fact, Jack."

Alysha frowned. "Mom said something happened in Annapolis. You and some old mobster."

Tommy felt his jaw tighten. "What she says to you, I don't know. What happened was I almost got in trouble for something down Annapolis, but I was lucky. I was in a car when somebody was killed, but I didn't kill him. I got no reason lie to you about that. I was never charged, so neither did the police believe I killed the guy."

The chaos in the casino grew louder. Somebody rushed into the bar and yelled out the jackpot, twelve million. Excitement filled the casino floor. Some of the people seated at the bar and the surrounding tables gathered near the railing to better view the commotion. Tommy waived the waitress over, paid the tab, and guided his daughter out of the bar. They walked the length of the casino floor to the Boardwalk exit and stepped outside. The mid-August sun was intense. Both father and daughter shielded their eyes.

"So, then how do you survive?" Alysha said. "How do you live?"

Tommy removed his hand and squinted from the sun's glare. He turned his head and felt a much needed ocean breeze. He made his way to the boardwalk railing, turned and leaned against it so the beach was behind him.

"Did you gamble last night?" Alysha said. "Where'd you get the money for that, never mind the escort?"

"I was playing a fie'dollar table, honey," Tommy said. "A big fifteen bucks a hand, the Let It Ride game, which I hardly ever did, leave up the fifteen. You have to know, I lost sixty-fie' dollars and walked. That's when I saw you." Tommy slid a hand across the iron railing. It was hot to the touch. He quickly removed it. "This fuckin' heat," he said. "Let's find some shade."

They walked along the beach side of the boardwalk toward the Ocean One Mall. Tommy used the back of his right wrist to wipe the sweat from his forehead. Alysha kept a hand up to shade her eyes.

"What's it about, these questions?" Tommy said. "I was gonna tell you another funny story, a real one happened last night before I saw you. True story."

"Another Honeymooner joke? Please, Dad."

"No, listen, it's funny. I'm out to dinner with some broad last night, she's not too bright. She's not sure what to order off the menu, this fancy place in there. She says to me, she says, 'Can you order my appetizer?' 'Sure,' I says. What do you like? Before she answers the waiter comes over to read the specials. He starts with something French, *Fromage Frais* he says, whatever the fuck that is. This broad, she looks at me like the guy just up-chucked his oatmeal on the table. She says to me, she says, do they have pictures?"

Alysha frowned.

"What? That's not funny?"

"Broad, Dad? Some broad?"

"Alright, she was an escort."

"Jesus Christ."

"What, you didn't think it was funny?"

"Not at all. Not the story or that you pay for sex."

"I paid for an escort. Was a business transaction. It's easier that way, a guy like me."

Alysha held both hands up, shook her head and said, "Fine. Whatever. Can we get back to—"

"You grilling me? Sure, that's how you want to spend our time, ga'head."

Alysha frowned.

"Well?" Tommy said.

"I always wondered," she said. "I'd heard stories growing up, but nothing about you being a killer."

"Jesus Christ, Alysha, because I'm not."

His daughter waited for more. "Look," he said. "We're Irish, right? So, I can't be a mobster, a Mafia guy. I knew some people were, and I got involved with a few of them, but that's it. Those were choices I made early on because I fucked myself by not going to school and doing the right thing when I was young. What you're doing now, what you've been doing since you was young, good in school and so on, that wasn't me. My fault, yes, but that doesn't mean I'm supposed to be somebody else's flunky, okay? You understand what I'm saying here?"

"You're justifying criminal behavior," Alysha said.

"Yeah, okay, I am, but you tell me the difference between that, what I did, and what these clowns in Washington do? What, those wars they send these kids off to die and get maimed in, that's for defense of country? Somebody attacking us we don't know about? They do that to protect the guys own them, the money behind the politicians. Then they made that law says they can do it forever, however much they want. Something United, whatever the fuck. Let's the real money in this country, not the mob, not the street criminals, the ones behind the corporations, those guys, they get to own the politicians outright, and everybody else gets to suck the wind they leave behind. Well, not me, okay. That bullshit isn't for me."

Alysha shook her head. "That's still justification, or are you telling me that what I'm doing is wrong, too? Going to school, being legitimate. Is that wrong?"

"No, because you're not looking to rule anybody. You wanna be a vet, right? You're looking to help animals. The fuck's wrong with that? These other clowns, the ones come from money, they could care less about you or the animals you save. They're in the game to keep control. Me, I'm not willing to be controlled. That's all I'm sayin' here."

They stood looking at one another a long moment. Tommy went to hug his daughter, but Alysha stepped back and said, "Mom told me this a few weeks ago, when she said you were a killer."

"She spewing this shit to your sisters?"

"No. Not that I know of. I don't think so."

"They're too young to hear shit like that. They won't know what to think."

"I'm sure she hasn't."

Tommy frowned, was about to say something else, then stopped to catch a breeze. He turned to face the ocean. "That feels better," he said.

"Maybe we should go back inside," Alysha said.

Tommy looked into his daughter's eyes. "What happened a few weeks ago?"

Alysha shook her head.

"Had to be somethin'," Tommy said.

"She got dumped."

"Who, the lawyer?"

Alysha nodded. "She blames you."

"Of course she does. Why'd she get dumped?"

"He found out about your past. He's planning to run for something. Some local political office or something, said he couldn't because of your past. Some newspaper learned about it."

"She never told him, that'd be her fault. What she gets for sleeping with a politician."

"He's not one yet, but that's her, Dad. I want to know from you."

"No, okay? The answer is no."

"Then how do you live? How do you earn money?"

Tommy wiped his forehead again. "I'm a consultant. You know that."

"I know that's a bullshit job you don't really do. And even if you did, how could you afford this place, Atlantic City? Coming here, I mean. Gambling the way I saw you last night, hookers. You're doing that as a consultant?"

"I could ask the same thing of you," Tommy said. He couldn't tell her the escort was a potential cover, or that he was in the hotel under one phony credit card, or that he'd used another phony card to hire the escort. Everything was a lie. "What're you doing here?" he said, "Since when you come to this place, Atlantic City? And she was an escort, not a hooker. There's a difference."

Alysha frowned. "There isn't a difference, except for the price. And I told you I'm here for a bachelorette party. I've been here twice in my life. I don't even like it here. And I wasn't gambling. I don't gamble. It's stupid."

"You're smarter'n me, except how did you see me playing cards, you weren't inna' casino?"

"We were walking through the casino to get to the nightclub."

Tommy smiled. She'd become the beautiful woman her mother was at the same age; twenty-two, tall and lean with blonde hair and blue eyes. She'd only disappointed him twice he could remember. The first time when she quit college after two years, then again when she told him she was engaged. She'd since returned to school and had dumped the fiancé. Now she wanted to be a veterinarian, something that couldn't make him more proud. He'd already put aside the cost for veterinarian school, but he couldn't give it to her yet, not without an explanation.

And here she was asking the questions he'd dreaded from the time her mother served him with divorce papers.

He guided her toward the mall again, taking slow steps as they walked. "You're asking me am I still dirty?" he said. "Yeah, a little, but I used to be a bartender and I have managed bars, so I'm not exactly running a scam with the consultant business. It's complicated, my life. I don't blame anybody for that. Like I said, it's my mess and I'll deal with it, but you're asking am I a killer. I said no, end of story. I won't say it again, so don't ask it again."

"I was hoping you'd be honest with me, Dad."

Tommy put a hand on his daughter's arm, felt the smooth skin, leaned in close and kissed her shoulder. "Those freckles," he said. "You're beautiful, kid."

Alysha didn't flinch. "Dad?"

Tommy sighed. "Honey, this is a world I don't fit. I can't explain it better'n that. I have issues, no doubt. We all do. Mine are more complicated. I don't believe in a world where men have to take it up the ass to earn a paycheck. I don't believe in being somebody's piss boy. Look at that shit happened in New York, was all over the news last month. Some poor bastard trying to feed his family selling cigarette lighters gets whacked because some punks with badges were playing cops and robbers, tried to make it so the guy was dangerous. That's how they justify it, not me. Their lives were in danger? Really?"

"The guy resisted arrest, Dad."

"Oh, please, Alysha, don't be so naïve. That's what you think that was, resisting arrest? The guy was a three-hundred pound slob couldn't tie his shoes without getting down on all fours. He look like he played the NFL to you? Their lives weren't in danger, okay? That can't be justification for every time some cop wants to prove he's a tough guy or gets nervous and shoots before they know what they're shooting about. Some overzealous punks decide they want to play tag team on some porker can barely wipe his ass, wouldn't last thirty seconds in a fight before he was out of breath. The way they took that guy down, he's tellin' them he can't breathe, that one guy leaning on his head like he was plugging a damn. He had to do that, put all that pressure in one spot, with three, four of his best friends helping him? The guy was onna' floor, couldn't breathe, tells them he can't breathe, and then he's dead."

"I'm sure they didn't want to kill him, Dad."

"Me, too, but they did. And then the one guy is on camera grabbing his crotch, waving to the person taking the video, mocking them. 'Look what I just did and you can't do shit about it.' The punk. That's what that looked like to me. Nothing but a punk, except he has a badge and a gun to make himself feel tough. That's our legal system today. Cops inna' right district, the DA has to work with them, nothing happens. Protests. Big fuckin' deal. Show's over, on to the next sucker. No thanks, honey. I'm not playing that game, and I'm not about to sell cigarette lighters to pay the freight. Why play by the rules, they're made to keep you inna' shit? The people condemn guys hustling to survive, they should see what it's like to earn seven-fifty an hour flipping burgers while the corporation owns the franchise, the pimps on the corporate board, they're off playing golf in Bermuda, banging their secretaries, whatever. Then they retire with multimillion dollar packages. Fuck that. No thanks."

Tommy raised both hands up in surrender. "Look," he said, "this world isn't fair. You don't know that yet, you will soon enough. That's nothing new or profound, but it's something I'm not willing to accept. I have one obligation, to make sure you and your sisters have enough to become independent. I'll protect you however necessary, including providing in whatever way is necessary. After that, you're all three on your own. Me, too, but that's my business. Okay?"

Alysha frowned. "Mom said you had a weird sense of right and wrong."

"Distorted is what she said. Distorted sense of right and wrong, and she's not the only one says it, but that too is my business. Now, what's going on with school? You accepted to a vet school yet or no? You could throw a fastball like this kid the Little League World Series, Mo'ne Davis, you'd have a full scholarship."

Alysha rolled her eyes. "I have another year," she said. "But I'm pretty sure I'll get accepted. My grades are good enough."

"And when it's time I'll have the money," Tommy said. "You'll apply for the loans and I'll feed you the cash to pay them, so no flags are raised. Not you or your mother have anything to say about that, how or where I get the money. That's my business. She says it's my fault she didn't mention the details to the latest love of her life? She ever tell the first guy? The one she married, that jerkoff? What was his name again?"

"Joe Collins."

"Right. She ever tell him who I was? Might've been a good idea, you know."

"Not until he got abusive. Then she did, yeah. To scare him."

Tommy stopped walking. "Abusive?"

Alysha tried to blow it off. "He was an asshole," she said. "We hated him from the day she brought him home. He liked to call us his stepchildren, but we never referred to him like that. He was Joe, that's it. Just Joe."

"She never told me about that either, her husband was abusive. He ever touch one of you, you or your sisters?"

Alysha looked away as she shook her head. "No, never."

"Hey, look at me."

Alysha faced him again. "No, he didn't. I swear it. He worked different shifts at the Domino factory. We hardly ever saw him."

He could tell she was holding back, probably because she still believed what her mother had told her.

"He didn't," she said again.

Tommy frowned. "Okay," he said, "then let's drop this shit for now. I was surprised to see you here last night, especially in that dress you painted on. I know it's been a few months."

"Five."

"Five. So, what say we go in the mall there, I buy you something to wear back to that yuppie school in New York doesn't look like you're hooking to pay the tuition? Maybe some perfume, too. So's it keeps the assholes away. That smell you're wearing now, that natural summer smell? Irresistible."

Alysha smiled. "That's what you used to say about Mom, that you loved her summer smell."

"Yeah," Tommy said, "I used to say that."

■ ■ ■

New Jersey/Pennsylvania

Back in his room, Tommy stood in front of the floor-to-ceiling windows and looked out over the Atlantic City Boardwalk and the Atlantic Ocean. It was another scorching day. The radio put the temperature at 92°. Tommy watched a lone jogger skirting the edge of the water on the beach, one man defying the heat. What happened if he passed out? The lifeguards weren't on duty yet. Who went to his aid? Would anyone watching him call for help?

Seeing there were no lifeguards on duty reminded Tommy of his father and how the old man had lost it one day when he caught a lifeguard sleeping in his chair. Tommy was no more than ten years old the day the family spent the afternoon at Gunpowder Falls, his father's favorite, and Tommy's father nearly toppled the lifeguard chair onto its side because anyone standing near it could hear the lifeguard snoring.

Edward Dalton had been an honest, hard-working man, with little tolerance for laziness. A union factory worker his entire life, Tommy's father had believed in and had pursued the American dream with great passion. A heart attack while working in 120° heat had killed Edward Dalton at the age of fifty-one. When the company won the lawsuit his mother had brought for poor working conditions on the factory floor where her husband died, Tommy lost faith in the system his father had believed in the length of his short life. Tommy had never committed a crime or ever considered one until after his mother's lawsuit was lost. When he was fired from a busboy job for yawning during a staff meeting, Tommy decided it was time to make his own way.

He took up with a local street gang involved in petty crimes until the day he was caught robbing a grocery store in the middle of the night. Instead of giving up his friends, Tommy took the pinch without snitching. He broke his prison cherry doing 8 of a 15-month sentence at the Baltimore City Detention Center. The Eager Street education he received there introduced him to lifelong street connections. Two days after his release, he was contacted by James "Gili" Thomasso, a Philadelphia mobster operating in Baltimore.

Tommy graduated from petty street crimes to collecting for loan sharks and bookmakers, occasionally working a hijacking score engineered through Gili. Then there was the Annapolis hit he'd assisted Gili on shortly before the old man retired. Once Gili left the life, Tommy became desperate enough to try a bank job that would cost him six years and his marriage.

He was still thinking about the guy jogging on the beach by himself without a lifeguard around as he reached for one of two burner cell phones to call his daughter. Alysha picked up after two rings.

"Hey," Tommy said.

"Hey," Alysha said.

"Where are you?"

"On my way to Mom's. Told you I was leaving."

"You driving now?"

"Yes. I'm stopping there and heading back to school."

"Then get off the phone before you get a ticket. Love you."

"Love you, too," she said.

He smiled thinking about how surprised he'd been walking into her in the casino last night. The tight red tube dress she was wearing was cut way too short for him not to say something; his first words in five months said in anger: "Are you fucking kidding me?"

"Hello to you, too, Daddy," Alysha had said.

"Never mind the sarcasm, lady. You look like a hooker. So do your friends. What the hell you doin' here?"

Five minutes of arguing ensued, at the end of which Tommy had her room number and a promise she'd call him from whatever club they were celebrating the bachelorette party at before she returned to her room. He didn't expect the call and was grateful when it came a few minutes before three o'clock in the morning.

Then this morning, out on the boardwalk, he'd lied through his teeth when she asked him if he was a killer. He couldn't believe what his ex-wife had told their daughter about him, but Sandi had always been vindictive. He should've known that sooner or later she'd want to hurt him. Their kids were her best weapon.

He prepped himself for work before the noon checkout. Tommy stood in front of the bathroom mirror, wet and brushed his red hair straight back, then covered it with a black curly wig. He turned sideways to make sure none of his red hair was visible, then sucked in his stomach enough to hurt. At forty-nine years of age, at six-foot, two hundred pounds, Tommy was still in good enough shape to do his job, so long as it didn't involve running or anything else athletic. He'd grown lazy the last few years, maintaining his weight through dieting, but ignoring the cardio regiment he'd once stuck to with a determined discipline.

He frowned at his reflection, then reached for his open pack of cigarettes—Camel regulars. He tossed them in the trash basket, finished dressing and made his phony checkout with a few minutes to spare. Ten minutes later he was crossing Pacific Avenue. He walked north on New York Avenue to Arctic Avenue, turned left to Kentucky Avenue, and then walked south back to the small strip mall off Atlantic Avenue where the CVS was located.

He'd been told that a Michael Givens had double-crossed what was left of the Philadelphia mob by moving prescription Oxycontin in Atlantic City. Tommy couldn't care less. Both parties were guilty of the same crime. Tommy had little use for either side, except one was paying him. He'd stopped asking questions a long time ago.

He believed what he'd told his daughter about politicians in Washington sending kids off to die for the sake of oil and defense contractors. The former Vice President, the same little shit who'd shot his friend in the face, had deferred going to Vietnam five times and had the nerve to defend sending other kids off to die. Tommy looked at cowards like that and believed they were a thousand times worse than he'd ever been. His work, whatever it entailed, was how Tommy got by, end of story.

The van was where he'd parked it two nights ago, alongside Brown Park on North Kentucky Avenue. He opened the back doors and stepped inside. He surveyed the street behind him as he closed and locked the back doors. He put on a pair of surgical gloves before removing a Mannlicher-Schoenauer hunting rifle from a rolled up rug. He set the rifle behind the console up front, then stepped over the console and started the van. He let the driver's window down a few inches, then stepped back behind the console and screwed on the sound suppressor. A few minutes after one o'-clock, Michael Givens stepped around the corner of North Kentucky Avenue. He was carrying a plastic bag by its handles. Tommy waited until Givens was midway across Arctic Avenue before he fired a single round. The bullet entered Givens' forehead above his right eye and exited the right side of his head, taking out most of the back of his skull with it. The body dropped in the middle of the avenue. Tommy set the rifle down, stepped over the console into the driver's seat, and then put the van into gear. He made a right onto Arctic Avenue as the light turned green. He checked his rear view mirror twice before taking Martin Luther King Boulevard to Baltic Avenue, then the Atlantic City Expressway toward Philadelphia.

Just under an hour later, under the Jersey side of the Walt Whitman Bridge, he spotted the white Chevy Impala parked alongside the parking lot. He drove to Essex Street, turned left and parked the van off the corner. He put the rifle in a large duffle bag, stepped out of the back of the van, took the duffle bag with him, relocked the doors, and walked around the corner to the Chevy Impala. He put the duffle bag in the Impala's trunk before getting behind the wheel. He opened the glove compartment and found an envelope thick with cash. He glanced inside the envelope, fanned the cash, saw they were hundred dollar bills, but didn't count them. He slid the envelope back inside the glove compartment, started the car, and then headed back toward an entrance to the bridge and Philadelphia. He'd skipped lunch and was hungry. He was thinking he'd have a cheese steak sandwich the city was famous for before heading to New York.

Staten Island, New York

Gasper Cirelli bent at the waist, leaned forward in the yard chair, and sucked a clam off the half shell. He squinted from the lemon he'd squeezed on the clam as he watched his eldest son retrieve two cold beers from a cooler across the yard. It was mid-afternoon. The sun was strong. The smell of chlorine from the pool was strong. Gasper stood up and maneuvered the table umbrella so it kept the sun off the plate of clams. He moved his chair closer to one of two fig trees, then sat back in his chair and watched as five of his six grandchildren played volleyball in the large in-ground pool.

Across the yard, his daughter and daughter-in-law sat under an awning near the far end of the pool. Gasper noticed a pitcher of wine in the middle of the table. Both women were smoking. Each had a glass of wine.

"Need more lemon?" Frank Cirelli asked his father before sitting alongside him in a yard chair.

"I'm good," Gasper said. "Your sister drinking again?"

"It's Sangria, Pop. Angie's watching out."

Gasper was wearing a wife beater t-shirt and grey shorts. Frank wore white shorts and a beige tank top.

"You talk to Adamo?" the old man asked.

Frank nodded. "Says he has somebody."

"Out of town, I hope."

"What he says."

"You measure the risk?"

"Nothing to measure. Farese gets on the stand, I'll have to wipe out an entire crew."

"You'll still have cleanup."

"I know."

The old man grabbed a quarter slice of lemon and squeezed it over a row of clams on a plate. He brought a clam to his mouth, stopped and said, "What I missed most I was away." He sucked the clam from the half shell, licked two fingers, and then wiped his mouth with the back of his right wrist.

Frank said, "You're worried about Adamo, I understand."

"Concerned, not worried."

"He's been good for us, but he's old now. How much more can he do for us? It's his time."

The old man pointed to a newspaper he'd been reading earlier. The headline read: *I'm choking! I'm choking!* "This bullshit," he said. "You see the video?"

Frank nodded.

"Five cops and one fat moolie," Gasper said. "Back in the day, they wanted him away from the store, they called us, not the cops. The fat fuck'd have a broken leg, but he'd still be alive."

Frank smiled. "And you'd make a deal, have him hawking for us," he said.

"Instead they break us up with all their deals and now you got young punks with badges making believe it's the wild-west, they gotta shoot a guy he looks at them the wrong way."

Frank sipped his beer, belched, then said. "And protests up the ass. Last time, that Zimmerman thing in Florida, took me three hours to get home. I was on the west side, didn't know they blocked up all of Times Square until it was too late."

The old man leaned forward on his chair. "I'm serious about the clean-up. Anybody knows about Farese, they'll have that chip to play down the road."

"I know. Everybody's on a short leash. No time to check and double-check. I get word somebody's about to turn, I even get a feeling, they're gone."

The old man nodded again. "Good," he said.

Frank held his beer bottle against his face. "Think we'll ever get a break from this heat?"

Gasper shrugged. He'd stepped out of the limelight six weeks before he began a ten year federal racketeering sentence. He spent the first five years in Terre Haute, Indiana, the last five years in Talladega, Alabama. He preferred living out the rest of his life at home, but there was no avoiding the counseling his son required.

He looked across the pool at his daughter. She was sucking down the Sangria way too fast.

Frank saw where his father was looking and said, "She's had it rough. I don't begrudge her getting numb once in a while."

Gasper frowned. His daughter had been through a lot. Losing a ten-year-old to a family cancer had been tough enough, but then her husband was pinched moving cocaine and immediately flipped. Fortunately, he was killed during a prison riot before he could testify against his brothers-in-law or anybody else.

Frank was Gasper's second son. His first boy, Gasper Jr., was dead at 43 from the same leukemia that had killed his nephew, Gasper's grandson. The old man had tried to keep his two younger sons, Frank and Paul, out of the life, but once his oldest died there was no way to keep the reigns without involving his blood.

Gasper wasn't happy about an associate Frank was about to use for an important job. Killing a cop, even a retired one, required the kind of professional Frank was ignoring. When he got out of prison, Gasper had hoped he'd live the rest of his life in relative peace, but Dominick Farese was a serious threat to several made members of their crime family.

Gasper lit the cigar he'd left in an astray alongside the plate of clams.

"You know the kid's too anxious, right?"

"He's twenty-five, Pop. Of course he's anxious."

"He's also a hot head. Thinks he's impressing me when he shoots his mouth off driving home."

"Feelin' his oats is all."

"He fucks this up, you'll have major heat. Not to mention he's untested."

"He fucks it up, I'll take care of it."

"Unless you can't get to him."

Frank took another long guzzle of beer, then belched into a fist. "'Scuse," he said.

"He's untested," Gasper repeated.

Frank nodded.

Gasper sat back in his chair and shrugged again. "Okay," he said, "but at least have somebody sitting on him."

Frank smiled at his father. "Ready for your coffee?"

Gasper stared at his son.

"Go fuck myself?" Frank said, still smiling.

"Good idea," Gasper said.

■ ■ ■

New Jersey

It was early evening when Tommy was on his way to New York. He could smell the fresh cut grass along a stretch of the New Jersey turnpike.

He took deep breaths and enjoyed the natural fragrance, one of the enjoyments he'd found in driving along turnpikes. He was close to Exit 7 when he dialed the number and pressed send on his disposable cellphone. He waited two rings before his ex-wife answered.

"Hello?" she said.

"You told Alysha I'm a killer?" Tommy said.

"Shit," Sandi said. "I should've known it was you. Soon as I didn't recognize the number, I should've known. This one of your burners you're calling from?"

Tommy was in the right lane on the New Jersey Turnpike heading north. He noticed an SUV riding his bumper and squinted at the rear view mirror.

"Hello?" Sandi said.

"Why would you tell Alysha something like that?" he said.

"Because it's true."

Tommy was eyeing the SUV in his rearview mirror.

"Hello again?" Sandi said.

"I'm here," Tommy said. "I don't get it, Sandi. You blow a marriage to some wannabe politician and you blame me. Fair enough, but why say something like that to our kid?"

"Yeah, well, it was because of you I blew that marriage, thank you very much."

"You should've told him about me. It's not my fault you didn't."

Tommy tapped his brakes a few times to back the SUV off.

"What do you want, Tommy?"

Tommy took his foot off the gas and braced himself in case the SUV hit him. He saw it jerk back a second, then speed up again. Then he heard the SUV's horn blowing and it pissed him off.

Tommy held up his middle finger.

"Hello?" Sandi said.

"Sorry," Tommy told Sandi. "I got an asshole on my bumper here."

"Why don't you shoot him?"

"Maybe I will."

"Look, I don't have all day, okay? What is it you want?"

The SUV's horn was still blaring. Tommy tapped his breaks again. The SUV finally swung into the left lane and pulled alongside Tommy. The driver was wearing a cowboy hat. He yelled curses at Tommy through an open passenger window. Tommy gave him the finger again. The SUV sped up to cut in front of Tommy, forcing him to hit his break. Then the SUV gained speed and distance, the driver holding up his middle finger this time.

"Asshole," Tommy said.

"Fuck you," Sandi said, then killed the call.

"Shit," Tommy said. He immediately hit redial and waited for his ex-wife to answer the phone. He started to count aloud after the tenth ring and made it to fifteen before Sandi picked up.

"What!" she yelled.

"I wasn't cursing you," he said. "It was the guy in the SUV."

"What do you want?"

"I want you to quit talkin' shit about me to our kids. I can only hope you're not talking this shit to anybody else."

"Or what?"

"Jesus Christ, Sandi. I'm not asking for anything special here. You fucked up and you're taking it out on me isn't fair. At least leave the kids out of it, especially Alysha. She has enough to worry about now. The kid is working on her degree."

"Excuse me. I forgot she's your favorite."

Tommy rolled his eyes.

"I told her the truth and you know it," Sandi said. "Blame yourself if you don't like what you are."

Tommy had gained on the SUV. He saw it was pulling into a rest area and immediately took his foot off the gas pedal to keep his distance. He turned into the same rest area and hung back to see where the SUV parked.

"Hey, asshole!" Sandi shouted.

Her yelling caused Tommy to remove the cellphone from alongside his ear. He glanced at it a moment, furrowed his brow, and then killed the call. He saw the SUV pull into a parking spot close to the rest area entrance. Tommy parked facing an exit. He wrapped a fist around the keys and stepped out of the car.

The driver of the SUV was a heavyset man, about six-foot. He wore a beige cowboy hat, dungarees and pointy cowboy boots. Tommy jammed two fingers inside his mouth, pushed his curled tongue back and forced a loud whistle. The cowboy turned toward the sound and Tommy waved at him.

"You like to ride bumpers?" Tommy said.

They were about ten feet apart when the cowboy recognized Tommy. "And you're the motherfucker likes to give the finger," the cowboy said. Tommy smiled as he continued approaching the big man. Then the cowboy squared off and started to cock a fist when Tommy stepped into a quick kick. The point of his sneakers nailed the cowboy in the crotch. There was a loud gasp as both the cowboy's hands reached for his crotch. Tommy watched him drop to his knees.

"What's that?" Tommy said.

The cowboy groaned.

Tommy looked up and saw a small crowd had gathered. He nodded at them, called the cowboy a child molester, and then headed back to his car. He was back on the turnpike heading north inside a minute.

■　■　■

Two hours later, Tommy stopped at a liquor store in Fords, New Jersey, and bought a case of Coor's Light. He was on his way to having lunch with his closest friend and associate, James Doc Adamo. It was hot and humid when Tommy stepped out of his car at Adamo's home a few blocks from the liquor store. Tommy hoisted the case of beer onto his right shoulder and headed up the stairs to his friend's front door. He rang the bell at the same time he could hear thunder rumbling up above. He rang the doorbell again and the front door opened.

"Top of the morning," Tommy told his friend.

Doc was a stocky man in his early sixties. He wore a Mets baseball cap to cover his receding hairline. He stared at Tommy a moment, then pointed to his watch.

"Morning ended a bunch of hours ago," Doc said.

There was another rumble of thunder, this one louder.

"You gonna invite me in or what?" Tommy said.

"I was hoping it would start pouring first," Doc said, then glanced up at the sky and stepped aside. "But I have a life. Might as well come in."

A pizza box was opened on the kitchen table.

"It's only an hour cold," Doc said. "You can heat it if you want."

Tommy set the case of beer on a kitchen chair, pulled an envelope from his front pants pocket, and set it on top of the beer. He grabbed a slice from the pizza box and folded it in half.

"Use a napkin, you ignorant Mick," Doc said.

Tommy tilted the pointed end of his slice over an empty spot in the box and let the oil drip while Doc counted the cash in the envelope.

"There's an extra three hundred in here," Doc said.

"For the lousy pizza," Tommy said. "Maybe buy yourself a better baseball hat while you're at it. That fuckin' team, should be embarrassed."

Doc grabbed a slice of pizza and sat at the table. He said, "The van was caught on a couple of cameras on Arctic Avenue. Bad move. On the other hand, the poor fuck lay in the street a good ten minutes before the cavalry arrived."

"What I was counting on," Tommy said, "nobody getting involved."

Doc bit into his slice and talked as he chewed. "You were lucky about that," he said.

"I walked into my daughter there," Tommy said. "My oldest, Alysha, couple nights before. Some bachelorette party. I swear the dress she wore was painted on. I says to her, I says, you fuckin' kidding me walkin' around like that? You lookin' to get raped?"

"She's of age, brother," Doc said.

"I don't give a fuck. I wasn't a happy man I saw her like that."

"Stands to reason. You patch it up?"

"I think so," Tommy said. "Who knows, but guess what her mother told her?"

"Shouldn't you be telling this to some professional?" Doc said. "Not that you're not giving me wood telling me your family problems, but I am more interested in your big rush to get this Atlantic City work done. That was a hasty fuckin' move. You're an ignorant Mick so I can understand the stupidity, but you're also a pro. You lose at the tables, need to get back out and earn?"

"I lost a few bucks," Tommy said.

Doc huffed. "You wanna throw money away," he said, "Frank Cirelli has a bookie in Coney Island'd be more than willing to take it."

Tommy knew Doc was referring to the bookie his brother had worked for before he was killed. Doc still held a grudge against the bookie, even though he took on work for the Cirelli crew from time to time. Lately he'd been providing untraceable guns and brokering hits for them. Tommy tried to joke his way around the bookie situation.

"What are you his runner?" he said. "You on a quarter sheet for Cirelli now?"

35

"Yeah, right," Doc said. "I was gonna grab action for some bookmaker, it wouldn't be for twenty-five percent."

Ten years ago Doc's brother was killed in a shootout with the police after being stopped with money he'd just collected for the Coney Island bookie. The police claimed Doc's brother was reaching for a gun he didn't carry when they shot him sixteen times. The newspapers had called it a shootout because of the gun Doc knew was planted on his brother. He never forgave the cops or the bookie his brother had worked for, but the guy who had set Eugene Adamo up was an inveterate gambler Tommy Dalton killed six months later. An unspoken favor, it had been a sloppy hit, something Tommy was later interrogated over because of a witness. It was the first and last time Tommy used a knife. Doc backed the witness down before an arrest warrant was issued, but Tommy's name had remained in the official case file.

"What was that guy's name again, the one in Coney Island?" Tommy said. "Cirelli's guy there?"

"Sal DeLuca," Doc said. "Prick goes by Sally. Sally D."

"Sally, huh?" Tommy said. "Figures. You eye-talians sure take to the fag nicknames."

Doc flipped Tommy the bird. "You should've waited," he said. "You could've avoided those cameras, shot them out or something. You're a dumb fuckin' potato head sometimes."

"What, and wait for you?" Tommy said. "Let you drive again? The man with no sense of direction?"

Doc spread his arms to his sides and made a fist, thumbs out. He wiggled his hands and said, "You forget how this country was discovered, I guess."

Tommy said, "Wasn't you, Guido."

"Was my people," Doc said.

"Right, your people. I forget you're a descendent from the fuckin' moron found America while aiming for India."

Doc used a fork to remove some melted cheese from the end of his slice. "There's a new piece of work, you want it."

"Maybe," Tommy said as he chewed on a bite of pizza. "The kid wants to be a vet. Can always use more cash."

"Hundred-K," Doc said. "Some guy inna' witness protection program, but you'd have to travel to get him."

Tommy rolled his eyes. "That's a lot of scratch, even for your Dagos."

Doc shrugged again. "Man's willing to pay it, I'd think you're willing to take it."

"Travel where?"

"I won't know until you commit, but you'll have to take the final meeting."

"The guy's a witness, it's high profile. What was the finder fee?"

"Depends where it came from, but your guess is as good as mine."

"Unless they're throwing figures around with no intention of paying them in full. Front some cash, even fifty, sixty percent, get the job done, and then get rid of everybody involved. It's high profile, it could go that way."

"If it's witness protection, I doubt they'd take that kind of risk. Something goes wrong, they're more fucked than they let the guy sing onna stand."

Tommy frowned.

"Up to you," Doc said.

"It's enough I could walk away from this shit once for all."

"What I was thinking."

"What's your end?"

"Twenty-five. All up front, but that's standard for me."

"Because you're special or needy?"

"Fuck yourself."

Tommy chuckled. "She told her I was a killer," he said. "You believe it? My ex, she doesn't even know that, not for sure, but that's what she tells the kid. She says to her, she says, your father is a murderer."

"She's pissed off," Doc said, "probably because her life's been shit since she tossed you. Or maybe she got her period. Forgetaboutit already."

"Alysha mentioned, hinted more like, her stepfather was abusive," Tommy said.

"Hinted or said?"

"She'd never tell me, although I think she started to."

"Because she's looking out for you, she didn't tell you," Doc said. "Let it go."

Tommy's eyebrows furrowed. "Some punk sniffing around my ex's snatch, he put his hands on my kids, I'm gonna' let it go?"

"You don't know he did anything. Who are you, Dexter all of a sudden?"

"The fuck's a Dexter?"

"Right," Doc said. "I forgot, you're above watching television."

"It's boring is why I don't watch it," Tommy said. "You're an old fuck got nothin' better to do."

"I can't argue with that," Doc said. "The kid say she was hit, abused, whatever? Alysha tell you that?"

"No," Tommy said.

"Then let it go. No reason inna world to whack the guy unless you're looking to get into the shit. And you'd be playing right into your ex's hands. You think she put one up your ass talkin' to your kid, imagine what she'd say to the law."

"I didn't say I was gonna whack him."

"I know how you think, like a caveman. Your fuckin' people, that potato famine. None of you geniuses ever thought to go fishing? It's a fuckin' island, for Christ sakes."

"Cute," Tommy said, "for a knuckle-dragger."

"Don't try and jerk my chain," Doc said. "I know how your distorted mind works. You don't redeem yourself by killing people."

Tommy placed little to no value on human life he didn't respect. Those he killed for money fell into that category, and he had no reservations. If there was a higher being and he had to pay for his sins, so be it, but he'd gotten into arguments about God more than once with Doc and hadn't changed his mind. Tommy believed there was one life to live and taking shit from anybody couldn't be a requirement. After getting out of prison, he'd stayed clean and poor while he was on parole, and then he turned a corner when he took out a lawyer who'd made the mistake of driving his sister to the point of attempting suicide, one of three Tommy had killed for reasons other than money.

He was down to eating the crust of his first slice of pizza. He bit into one end and spoke while he chewed. "Seriously, you need to find another pizza joint," he said.

"Right, ignore me," Doc said. "Then make it your business to walk away from a job you can milk for cash so's you can shoot some jerk-off who may or may not have abused your kids."

"Now I know why your wife went back to work," Tommy said.

Doc flipped him the bird again.

Tommy reached for another slice. "We know who's going down?"

"No," Doc said. "You could pay attention a minute, focus on the money instead of your temper, you'd've heard me the first time. No, we don't. They're waiting on us to commit."

"And I have to travel," Tommy said.

"What the man said."

"That means unchartered waters," Tommy said. "No time to get familiar with the place? No. No time to investigate a few variables? No. And I'm working for people I can't trust. Your people. Let's-make-a-dealers."

"They pay in green," Doc said, "That's all that counts, no?"

"They're not your friends. You shouldn't be so anxious to accommodate them."

Doc leaned back, smiled and said, "You shouldn't be a moron, but you can't help yourself. You take the work, we'll meet at the used car lot on Hyland Boulevard."

"Same place as last time?"

"It's good, don't worry." He saw Tommy was smiling and said, "Dumbass."

Tommy chuckled.

Doc stared, waiting out Tommy until he felt it and looked up.

"What?" Tommy said.

"You're gonna whack that guy bothered your kids," Doc said.

Tommy shrugged.

"Sometimes I wonder you're not tired of living, kid," Doc said. "I mean it."

"I'll wait until after the job, it makes you feel better," Tommy said. "That okay with you?"

Brooklyn, New York

Quinlan King recognized the waiter from the restaurant on Mulberry Street as soon as the Sonata pulled up to the curb. The waiter tried to look tough after he beeped the horn. King stepped off the curb into the street and leaned forward as the passenger window was lowered.

"You King?" the driver said.

"I might be."

"You have our package?"

King smiled as he stood up. The waiter beeped the horn again and King continued on his way toward the deli to pick up breakfast, a fried egg sandwich and two cups of coffee. He heard the waiter curse behind him before he heard the Sonata's tires burning rubber as it sped up to the corner. King eyeballed the waiter before stepping inside the deli on Benson Avenue.

His order was waiting for him. He paid, picked up a Daily News, and headed back home. He walked to Bay 32nd Street, turned left and headed toward 86th Street. The Sonata sped ahead one more time. The waiter parked off the corner and was out of the car to wait for King on the sidewalk.

"You fucking with me?" he said as King approached.

"No wonder you guys have become a reality TV joke," King said.

"Excuse me?"

"Listen up, Guido. I'm going to walk to my house and sit down and have breakfast. When I'm done with that I hope to take a good, long, shit. One that'll make me feel ten pounds lighter. Then I'll wipe my ass, wash my hands real good, something I'm sure you never do after taking a duke. Maybe you wipe them on your pants or your mother's curtains. I'll step outside and make believe I'm checking the mail I forgot to get yesterday after drying my hands. While I'm out there checking for mail, I'll probably look to my right in the rose bushes we have. I hope to see a gym bag there. I'll take it inside and see there's something in it. If there is, I'll probably go for another walk, Eighty-sixth Street this time, maybe pick out some fresh fruit like your ancestors used to do before they all became gangsters. Then I'll see that piece of shit you're driving pull up to the McDonald's on Eighty-sixth. I'll take my time making sure there's nobody watching, then I'll either hand off what you're looking for, or take the train into the city and hope that dump I ate at yesterday has a waitress without a mustache. How's that work for you?"

The waiter glared at King. It was what King missed most since his retirement, being a cop in the organized crime unit and having the ability to insult mobsters and wannabes because there was nothing they could do about it. In this case, having something they wanted, it was no different, and King wasn't about to pass on the opportunity to fuck with this wannabe.

"You need to work on that tough guy stare," he told the waiter. "In the meantime, I'll assume you have no more authority than the flunky you are, and I'll leave you here to contemplate whether or not some old man is about to fuck you out of a hundred grand in Mob money. You'll start to wet your pants in five or ten minutes, but chances are you'll wait it out, realize I've got you by the balls no matter how you slice it. Until then, moron, have a nice fuckin' day."

"Fuck you," the waiter said.

"Now that you got that routine off your chest, I'll see you out front of that McDonald's I mentioned in another hour or so. Maybe longer."

The waiter continued glaring as King sidestepped him and continued walking around the block.

Half an hour later, King was counting the stacks of hundred dollar bills in the small bag he found between his rose bushes. Ten stacks of ten thousand dollars was the final count; one hundred thousand dollars in cash, half the score. King went up to his bedroom and stashed the money in the floor safe in his closet. He placed an old .38 on the top of the money before closing and locking the safe. He printed out the information he'd be turning over, folded and put the papers inside the pages of a paperback book he'd read a few years ago, then set the alarms for his house and walked to 86th Street.

He met a neighbor as he turned the corner onto 86th Street, a woman a few years younger than him he'd imagined was one hell of a looker thirty years ago. A divorcee always on the prowl, but way too close to home, JoAnne Razeli did her best to try to start a conversation with King. He told her he had an appointment two times before getting fed up and ignoring her outright.

"Fuck you," he heard her say as he walked away.

"Charming," he said.

She flipped him the bird Italian style, smacking the crook of her left elbow with her right hand.

King chuckled one more time before proceeding on his way.

■ ■ ■

Baltimore Highlands, Maryland

"Where are the twins?" Alysha Dalton asked her mother.

She was back home for an overnight with her sisters. She set two plastic bags from a Giant grocery store on the kitchen table. Sandi Dalton-Collins stared at her daughter through the smoke from her cigarette. Alysha removed two containers of milk, a loaf of bread and a jar of peanut butter. She put the milk in the refrigerator and was putting the peanut butter in one of the cabinets when she repeated her question.

"Hello to you, too," Sandi said.

Alysha wasn't in the mood for a fight. She closed her eyes and said, "Ma?"

"They're at Grandma's."

"Thank you."

Sandi crushed out her cigarette, stood up from the table and removed the peanut butter from the cabinet. "This goes with the cereal," she said. She moved the peanut butter to another shelf in the same cabinet.

"Sorry," Alysha said, "and you're welcomed that I picked it up. The girls said we ran out two weeks ago."

Sandi returned to her chair at the table and sat. "Have a good time with your father?"

Alysha said, "Not now, okay?"

"He called, you know."

"You have a nice conversation?"

"Don't get smart with me."

Alysha grabbed a Diet Coke from the refrigerator and sat across from her mother at the table.

"I can't believe you told him what I said," Sandi said.

"And he can't believe you told me what you said," Alysha said.

"Because it's the truth."

"Good. Maybe you should've told your lawyer the truth."

"I should've known you'd take his side."

"Yeah, well, I remember you takin' that asshole ex-husband of yours' side once, too."

"And I threw him out as soon as I knew what he did."

"Except you had to have proof. You didn't believe me."

Alysha had caught him in her bedroom going through her underwear, holding them up to his nose and smelling them. He'd been drunk and tried to pay Alysha to keep quiet. When she told him to get the fuck out of her room, he grabbed her ass on his way out of the bedroom, telling her that her mother would never believe her anyway, so he might as well get a grab. Alysha had slammed and locked the door behind him.

"I threw him out, didn't I?" Sandi said. "Your father would've killed him."

"So, what, you were protecting Dad? Please. You were embarrassed is what happened. If it wasn't for the twins telling you, he'd still be here, the pervert."

Both of Alysha's sisters, eleven year old twins, claimed they'd been grabbed by Sandi's husband when Alysha asked them if he'd ever done anything to them. Then Sandi threw the bum out and filed for divorce.

"And we had a chance to have a better life if it wasn't for your father," Sandi said. "I hope you realize that while you're assigning blame, Alysha."

Alysha stared at her mother a long moment, then shook her head.

"What?" Sandi said. "I'm wrong? He's a convicted felon."

"Daddy's right, you can't help yourself."

"Oh, great, Alysha, just great. Take the side of a murderer. I hope that helps you sleep at night."

Alysha put her hands up, then stood up from the table. "Okay, I'm done. I'll stop at Grandma's on my way back to school. I'll see the twins there."

"Fine, go."

"I am. And you're welcome for the groceries."

"And you're welcome for the roof over your head while your father was in jail, you little shit."

"Bye, Mom."

Alysha didn't make it to the car before the first tears streamed down her face.

■ ■ ■

Manhattan, New York

After changing locations a few times, Tommy met with Frank Cirelli in Riverside Park in Manhattan. It was a humid night, the air thick with a briny smell from the Hudson River. A small group of young white kids played soccer with a beach ball under the lights above a patch of lawn across from 116th Street. Three women, all of them au pairs, sat watching the kids from a nearby bench.

Tommy wore a curly black wig and sunglasses. He noticed Cirelli's hair was also dark and curly and smiled at the ironic twist. He handed the mob boss half of the pretzel he'd bought off a frankfurter vendor a few minutes earlier.

"I hope you like salt," Tommy said.

Cirelli used two fingers to remove some of the salt from his half of the pretzel, then took a bite from one end. "I hope you enjoyed making me dance," he said. "Go here, go there, it's not as easy as you think. I'm busy as it is. Sunday nights are supposed to be for family."

"I thought you'd appreciate the extra effort," Tommy said. "All that dancing, you eventually coming here, to the yuppie West Side? I know I feel safer. And it's still early enough." He glanced at his watch. "It's just eight o'clock now."

Cirelli watched one of the kids kick at and miss the beach ball. He said, "Except maybe I'm wearing a wire," he said, "you didn't pat me down. For all I know, maybe you're wearing the wire."

"Up to my asshole," Tommy said. "You want, I'll drop my pants, you can check. I'm not the shy type."

Cirelli looked past Tommy at the au pairs. "No thanks," he said. "Lou got your name from your friend. I was told you can be a smartass Mick, but you get the job done. That's all I care about."

"Must piss you off, a WOP having to hire a Mick. It's not like you don't have your own people. Useless as the day is long, I'm sure, but there they are, all those goombahs playing cards all day. It true they go those half-assed casinos used to be horse tracks?"

Cirelli had taken another bite from the pretzel. "You want to try a few more insults or get down to business? I have a long drive home tonight. Between these fuckin' protests and the work they're doing on the tunnel, I'll be lucky I get home before dawn."

"Sure, so long's I can assume we're settled on price," Tommy said. "Outside of expenses."

"I already told Doc," Cirelli said. "A hundred thousand, half and half."

"I'm more comfortable with sixty-forty," Tommy said.

"And I'd go for that if this were a ten dime job, but it's not. It's a hundred-k. So, fifty-fifty."

Tommy guided Cirelli farther west toward the Hudson River. "Who's the mark?" he said.

"Timothy Kline, his new name. He's on some island off the coast of New Hampshire. Some environmental island with only two ways to get there, boat or helicopter. They got a boat goes there every couple days, some ferry from Portsmouth, but that also brings tourists back and forth. Has something to do with arts and crafts classes. There's people, though, between the other workers and the visitors, it can get crowded."

"Expenses'll be high, I gotta charter a boat," Tommy said. "I'll need more up front."

"Or you could bring a friend knows how to steer one, rent something off a marina up there, whatever," Cirelli said. "Keep expenses low."

"I could hack into the pentagon and fire a missile, too," Tommy said. "Maybe put an ad in the paper."

Cirelli shrugged. "I'm just saying. It's not my problem."

"Well, since it's mine, the problem, make it sixty-forty."

"Another ten grand? You intend to buy a boat?"

"Whatta' you care it's not your problem?"

Cirelli paused a moment before he nodded. "You'll have everything you need tonight. See your friend. It's best not to waste time with this, so the sooner the better."

"The money's there, consider it done."

"Excuse my lack of enthusiasm about it being done. I prefer to wait and see."

"While you're waiting, ever hear of an incentive bonus?"

Cirelli shook his head. "You're a real shakedown artist," he said. "Okay, fine, but it's a one shot deal. Get it done tomorrow. I'll front sixty."

"I gotta hear you say it," Tommy said.

"Sixty-forty," Cirelli said.

Tommy took another bite from his half of the pretzel, then walked away north along the river.

■ ■ ■

Staten Island, New York

James Doc Adamo loaded Tommy Dalton's tools inside the front passenger side rocker panel of a 2012 Chevrolet Malibu. He added two fully loaded clips, a Gemtech Blackside-45 sound suppressor, and the Glock 21 Tommy favored, each wrapped in bubble packaging for stability. Adamo then sealed the rocker panel with duct tape, leaving a six inch cut of thin cable tucked under a strip of tape for Tommy to remove the panel.

Adamo also had a Ruger LCP 380 for Tommy, something easy to conceal inside his waistband or pocket. It was a backup gun in the event of a close range situation, the same type of weapon Adamo had once used to kill a carjacker in the South Bronx six years ago. That night he and his wife were on their way to visit family in New Rochelle and had to pass through a section of the Bronx on the entrance ramp to the Bruckner Expressway where stoplights provided easy pickings for carjackers. Adamo was talking to his wife after stopping at the light when two Hispanic men attempted the carjack. The one on his wife's side of the car was pointing a 9mm. The one on Adamo's side held a telescope baton and was threatening to break the window. The doors were locked and the windows up. Adamo's wife screamed. Adamo leaned to his left as if he were going to unlock and open the door, but removed the Ruger LCP 380 from an ankle holster instead. He turned to his right and fired twice through the passenger window. The first shot struck the man with the gun in the forehead, killing him instantly. When he turned to his left, the man with the telescope baton was sprinting in the opposite direction. There were cars behind his, but Adamo drove when the light turned green. He watched in his rear view mirror as the next several cars, although they paused for a few seconds, continued through the intersection and up onto the Bruckner Expressway.

The incident was never reported. Although in shock at the time, Adamo's wife of thirty-two years was more concerned with the incident being reported than the fact her husband had shot and probably killed someone. The next morning, when they watched the news report about the shooting, the police were still appealing to possible witnesses. It took a few more days before Maria Adamo could accept their good fortune.

Adamo was thinking about his wife as he waited for the money drop. Recently Maria had developed a taste for whiskey sours. It started at a wedding they'd attended a few months earlier. He made a mental note to stop at the liquor store the next day on his way for bagels. He'd get the whiskey sour mix and make a pitcher for her.

He was starting to get bored when one of Frank Cirelli's Brooklyn captains, Lou Testa, drove his Cadillac SUV into the lot. Testa had a young guy with him he introduced as the son of a close friend.

"Luke Palmieri," the gangster said. "Good kid working his way up. Part-time waiter in Little Italy, full time womanizer all over the place. What he says. I don't know I believe him about the broads, though. Never seen him with one yet."

Adamo remained on Testa's side of the car. He nodded at Palmieri instead of leaning in and accepting the hand shake extended to him.

Testa frowned at the insult, then turned to Palmieri. "Just breaking your balls, kid," he said. "Don't mind this old fuck, he don't have no manners is all."

"You're thin-skinned, you're in the wrong business," Adamo said to

Palmieri.

Palmieri looked away.

"He can handle it," Testa said. "Your guy all set?"

"Waiting on you," Adamo said.

Testa got out of the car and walked to the back. He used his remote to open the trunk. He removed two envelopes, one thicker than the other, beneath the spare tire cover and handed them to Adamo.

"Count it," he said.

"Nope," Adamo said.

"Nope? Why not?"

"One's not mine," Adamo said.

"So what? He's your guy, right?"

Adamo noticed Palmieri was out of the car now too. "Don't worry," Adamo said. "If it's not all there, either envelope, you'll get a call to come pick them back up. Which reminds me, about the other guy, the rest of it."

"Cash on delivery, right?"

"Cash where? Here? Someplace else?"

"Don't worry, you'll get it."

"Where?"

"Here, okay? We'll bring it here."

Testa looked at Palmieri and shook his head. "*Testa dura*," he said. Palmieri smiled.

"*Avete mezzo cervello, avrete gli chiedi di farvi scendere alla prossima Burger King si passa. Entra, compilare una domanda, e ricominciare da capo, ragazzo*," Adamo said, then turned to Palmieri and translated: "You have half a brain, you'll ask him to drop you off the next Burger King you pass. Go in, fill out an application, and start over, kid."

Testa flipped Adamo the bird. "Have a good night," he said.

Adamo ignored Testa and winked at Palmieri. He watched and waited until Testa drove out of the lot. He waited an extra minute, then headed inside the office, set the envelope on his desk, took a seat behind the desk, and then called Tommy Dalton. Twenty minutes later, Tommy pulled into the lot. When he stepped inside the office, Tommy was carrying a small gym bag.

"The Malibu?" he said.

Adamo nodded. "You need coffee?"

"No, I'm good. What you give me?"

"Forty-five. Glock."

"Punching power."

"You never know."

"Extra clip?"

"Plural. That means more than one."

Tommy smiled. "What about the car? My car."

"I'll drive it off tonight. Leave it my sister-in-law's place until you get back."

"Good. Thanks."

Adamo pulled the Ruger from his front pants pocket and set it on Tommy's envelope filled with cash. "You have a plan once you're there?" he asked.

"Fishermen," Tommy said. "I spent some time on the Google after you called. There's a marina runs boats out to the island. Local fishermen dock there. Lobstermen mostly, from what I found. They mention the balance?"

"Claims they'll bring it here again."

Tommy frowned. "I don't know I trust them on that. We should be prepared."

Adamo nodded.

Tommy picked up the envelope, then the Ruger. "Okay, then. I should head up."

"Hold on," Adamo said. "You speak to your daughter?"

"Yeah, why?"

Adamo paused a moment. "Okay, try not to get lost. I'd tell you to hug the coast, but then you might wind up some potato field."

Tommy grabbed his crotch.

"Be careful," Adamo said. "I mean it."

"Don't get teary-eyed on me."

Doc shook his head. "Fuck off."

"I'll see you when I see you."

Doc winked. "Not if I see you first."

■　■　■

Frank Cirelli parked in a lot off Father Capodanno Boulevard in Midland Beach. It was still early in the morning, but the sun was strong. He wiped sweat from his forehead with the back of his right hand as he made his way to the boardwalk. Last night had been tough putting up with the mouth on the Irishman he'd contracted the work to on Dominick Farese. Then when he finally made it home after all the traffic on the BQE and Staten Island Expressway, there was his wife waiting to break his balls about an argument their youngest had had with the old man again. Frank knew his father meddled in their parenting, but there was nothing to do about it. Gasper Cirelli was old school, very set in his ways, and completely unreasonable when it came to parenting. The old man never took guff from his kids and he wasn't about to take it from his grandchildren.

"An old asshole, your son called him, and I don't blame him," Frank's wife had yelled when Frank walked in the house. "He probably ran away again."

"The fuck are you talking about?" he said.

"Your father and Paul again. They fight like cats and dogs, and I can't take it anymore. I wish you'd tell him not to come here unless you're home."

"Yeah, right. Like that's gonna happen. Where's Paul now?"

"I don't know, he ran out. Your father called him a little faggot again, and then Paul called him an old asshole, which he is, and then Paul ran out."

"Call his cell."

"I already did. He won't answer. I left two messages. I'm sick of the fighting with those two. You need to keep him from coming here and starting shit. He's always starting something with Paul."

"I had a shit day, Angie, okay? Back the fuck off."

"You mean you didn't stop for a blow job somewhere? Am I supposed to feel bad?"

Frank stared at her until she was uncomfortable. "What?" she said.

"He probably went to his friend's house again. Did you call?"

"Your father called him a little faggot again."

"You said. Did you call his friend?"

"No, I didn't. I called his cell. I told you that. I just told you that."

Frank thought about cracking her one. He went to the basement instead. He ignored whatever wisecracks she was making behind him as he poured himself bourbon neat in a rocks glass. He took a few sips while she continued yelling, then he used the remote to turn on the television and watch ESPN for scores. He'd bet a dime reverse on his way home with his office in Coney Island—the Mets +120 IF to the Braves -120. He turned up the volume and sat in his recliner. Caught up in the story about a 13

year old girl named Mo'ne Davis pitching a shutout in the Little League
World Series earlier in the week, Frank sipped his drink until it was finished and his eyes grew heavy.

This morning he was stiff from spending most of the night in the recliner. He moved to the bedroom sometime after one o'clock in the morning and then the alarm woke him at six. Two cups of espresso later, he was
on his way to meet his father.

Now he spotted Gasper sipping coffee on the boardwalk in Midland
Beach. His father wore a Yankees sun visor and sun glasses. His skin, already dark, appeared weather beaten under the wife beater t-shirt he
wore.

"The guy Doc Adamo put us onto, he's a wiseass Mick cocksucker,"
Frank told his father.

"Good morning to you, too," Gasper said. He tapped the bench alongside him for Frank to sit.

"Makes it a lot easier to take care of the other guy, I'll tell you that much,"
Frank said as he sat alongside his father.

Gasper removed his sunglasses and turned to his son. "Who shit in your
cereal?"

"The prick I gave the work to last night, for one thing. Then Angie,
soon's I walked in the door. You gotta' lay off Paul, Pop."

"Lay off my ass," Gasper said. "You know what he called me?"

"After you called him a faggot? He's your grandson, for Christ sakes.
You're supposed to spoil him, not call him names."

"He's spoiled enough. It's time to toughen him up."

"By calling him a faggot? Do me a favor, please. Apologize to the kid."

"Yeah, right."

Frank shook his head.

Gasper smiled. "Angie got her twat twisted again? That was this is
about?"

"You enjoy breaking her balls, but then she breaks mine soon's I walk
in. Give it a break already. I'm the one catches it."

"Fine," Gasper said. "I'll apologize, but not to her."

Frank smiled. "I wouldn't ask you do that, not to Angie."

"Broad hates me."

"I think she hates me more."

Gasper faced the water again. "The guy leave yet?"

"He picked up what he needed. I assume so."

"He gets it done, you need to take care of him before the old man."

"I'm hoping to get it done the same time."

"Somebody reliable?"

"According to Testa."

Gasper nodded. "Don't miss."

"It was me, I wouldn't. It'll go a long way the Mick gets it done. We can use the boost."

"Your brother'll be happy, I know that much."

Frank nudged his father with his leg. "Might be time, after this is done, you talk to Paul."

"I said I'd apologize."

"I mean my brother, your son."

Gasper turned to Frank again. "You come here to break my balls this morning?"

Frank patted his father on the back. "I took a shot."

Gasper still refused to speak with his youngest son, Paul. Frank's brother had disgraced the family in a way that couldn't be forgiven. Brothers didn't fuck their sister-in-laws, not in a way they'd get caught. Frank wanted to kill his wife and brother when he learned about it from a cop with the organized crime unit, but Gasper had taken control of the situation by having Frank arrested and held in a holding tank while he took care of the mess. The brothers eventually patched things up, but Paul was still exiled to Florida as far as their father was concerned.

"You eat yet?" Gasper asked.

"No. You hungry?"

"I can eat. You buyin?"

"You're gonna apologize to your grandson, sure. I think I can find some coin for a breakfast."

Gasper winked at his son. "Then let's go already. My stomach's growling and in another few hours that criminal fuck reverend'll tie up every road on the island with ten thousand of his best friends, be no way to drive anywheres."

Frank stood up and reached a hand out to his father. He pulled the old man up off the bench. The two started walking.

"You know he was a rat for the feds, right?" Gasper said. "I mean besides he don't pay no taxes."

Frank was confused. "Who?"

"That bullshit reverend makes all the noise on television."

"That for real or alleged?"

"What are you, on his side now?"

"No, but I got bigger problems my own right now."

They were almost at the doors to the restaurant when Gasper stopped and turned to his son. "And that wife of yours, she hates me because of what I said once, I was drunk. She overheard and never forgave me."

It had to do with Gasper telling one of his friends that his new daughter-in-law, once she was pregnant, had grown a bigger ass than could fit in a normal sized chair.

"You ever apologize for what you say she overheard?" Frank said.

"The hell for? She didn't even know I knew she heard."

Frank rolled his eyes and said, "How 'bout we just get something to eat now?"

The old man frowned first, shrugged, then nodded. "Yeah, okay."

"Thank you," Frank said.

He opened the door for his father and rolled his eyes again when the old man had passed him on the way inside.

PART II

Rye Harbor, New Hampshire

Special Agent in Charge, Peter Billings, watched as a helicopter landed in the center of the paved parking lot across from the row of vendor shacks selling fishing trips and tours to Star Island. Billings wore a Boston Bruins baseball cap low on his head to shield his eyes from the bright sun. A gaunt man in his early sixties, Billings was looking at two more years to retirement and the easy life he'd once promised himself; early mornings watching the news over breakfast, catching a movie on Netflix in the afternoon, some afternoon reading, a nap, a home cooked dinner, and cheap Bruins season tickets at the TD Garden before a peaceful night of rest.

This morning a phone call woke him at quarter after six, one hour after the body of a witness under federal protection had been found dead in the back of a work shed on a tiny island off the New Hampshire coastline. He'd been asleep less than three hours, but it had been a deep sleep, the kind Billings only seemed to experience after a round of sex with his wife of thirty-five years. What made it worse than he was feeling now, standing outside on a 95° day, was that the phone call had also woken his wife.

"Who is that on the phone?" she'd asked.

He'd held up a hand twice to keep her from speaking, but once he heard the words "dead witness on our hands," Billings knew his chance for more sleep was over.

"You have to be kidding?" Claire Billings had said after he explained.

"I'm not," Billings said. "I have to go."

"He's dead already, he'll be dead when you get there, no matter when you get there," she said. "And don't they have other people junior to you they can bother at all hours of the night?"

"It's not the middle of the night, Claire. It's morning. Early morning, but still morning."

"Oh, bullshit, Peter," his wife said. "You don't get up until after nine most days now."

He explained the best he could while getting dressed, but his wife was still angry when he left their house in Cambridge. He'd headed straight for a Dunkin' Donuts, where he had to wait on a long line of cars for two medium-sized containers of black coffee and two old fashioned donuts. After his stop for coffee, the drive to Rye Harbor, New Hampshire, took him just under an hour.

He used the woods off the side of Harbor Road to relieve himself a few times while waiting almost two hours for the charter boat to take him to the island. The boat ride was another twenty minutes on a calm sea, during which he took a ten minute nap, but once he was on the island, the sun had come up and was beating down hot. With little breeze it had been stifling.

The victim, Timothy Kline, a.k.a. Dominick Farese, was lying face down alongside a work shed behind the biggest building on Star Island, the Oceanic House. Farese had been executed, no doubt about it. Two bullet holes behind his right ear were obvious enough to rule out all other forms of homicide. There was little doubt it was a mob hit, but how the killer managed to get on and off the island without being seen was the mystery.

Billings interviewed the island manager while they looked over the crime scene, an area behind a large work shed. The manager claimed he didn't know the victim was in the witness protection program. Billing wasn't sure he believed him.

After inspecting the shed area for half an hour or so, Billings was relieved when a helicopter dropped off a much younger agent with the same last name as a hockey player for the Tampa Bay Lightning, one of a few Florida teams Billings hated ever since his first wife moved to Florida with their only kid a few years ago.

Billings took the helicopter trip back to Rye Harbor, where he took an hour long nap in his car with the motor and air conditioning running. He ate a fish sandwich from one of the vendors, washed it down with a Diet Coke, then two bottles of water before he received word that the helicopter was on its way back from Star Island.

He was shading his eyes as the young special agent made his way from the helicopter across the parking lot.

"Anything?" Billings asked when they were a few feet apart.

Special Agent Robert Callahan shook his head. "A woman working the desk in the big building said nobody approached her about Farese, but she said she saw him come down through the lobby about four o'clock in the morning. She doesn't know why. She knew him as Timothy Kline. Said there was one girl working there Kline had been involved with. College kid. She was off this week, home for a wedding."

"Anybody hear anything?"

"Nothing."

"We searching the coastline for the boat?"

"Coast guard is on it," Callahan said. "The guy runs the place mentioned cameras in Portsmouth, where most of their people come and go from, the ferry there. This here, where we are now, is the alternate route, Rye Harbor."

Billings yawned into a fist. "Yeah, he told me the same thing," he said. "Whoever did this didn't go anywhere near Portsmouth. He probably came from here, right here, which is why I want the coastline searched. There'll be a boat adrift somewhere unless it was docked. They'll probably find the poor S.O.B. who piloted the thing, unless he was dumped in the water on the way back. A guy could launch a boat from anywhere nearby, but then he'd be off the beaten track and might not see the lighthouse across from the island. Had to be somebody knew the waters. Chances are we'll be finding him and his boat. This was a contract job. Somebody got paid to whack Farese. We don't have to guess too hard to figure out who footed the bill, but the question remains, who gave him up? My guess is it's somebody on that island, tourist or staff, recognized him. Had to be."

"That could take some time looking into everybody who visited or worked the island since Farese's there. It's the end of August now, that's two plus months. Could take us forever to interview everybody's been here."

Billings offered his hand. Callahan took it. Billings said, "Welcome to organized crime."

■ ■ ■

Portsmouth, New Hampshire

By four o'clock in the afternoon, with the temperature still hovering above ninety degrees and the air thick with humidity, Billings held a cold compress to his forehead in the lobby of the Sheraton Portsmouth Hotel. The agents had driven to Portsmouth from Rye Harbor. Callahan was on his cell phone just outside the lobby. He wasn't big, but Billings could see Callahan had broad shoulders and a thick neck to match a thick head of dark hair. Billings liked working with new agents, mostly because they didn't know enough to be cocky. Most were too scared to get in the way. It was one way to control a situation, having a rookie to shepherd through the investigative process.

Callahan was out of Concord, New Hampshire, what Billings knew about him. Four years a detective there before applying to the Bureau. He'd been a marine in Iraq before joining the police force. He was still a newlywed, at least by Billings' standards—an All-American boy turned soldier, turned man, turned cop, turned special agent.

Hopefully he wouldn't be a pain in the ass, Billings thought as he watched the young agent holding a cell phone to his right ear. Callahan was shaking his head on the other side of the hotel lobby glass. To his left, Billings could see the news vans setting up in the Isle of Shoals parking lot. He frowned at the sight. The swarm of publicity the murder on Star Island had attracted was exactly what the Mob wanted.

He turned and saw Callahan heading his way through the lobby doors. The young agent excused himself before sidestepping an obese woman heading for the doors.

Billings pointed at the door when Callahan was in front of him. "Good move," he said. "She might've crushed you."

Callahan glanced over his shoulder. "That's a bit harsh," he said.

Billings shrugged.

"You okay?" Callahan asked.

"Headache," Billings said. "What the Coast Guard have to say?"

"Abandoned lobster boat. The *Crustacean Queen*. Body in the forward cabin. If it's the owner, he's a family man."

"Shit."

Billings stood up from the chair he'd been sitting on. "Matter of time before somebody calls in for the guy," he said. "It's the owner, they'll know soon enough from the boat's ID."

"Glad I don't have to make that call," Callahan said. "Nothing worse."

"We're heading to Logan. Locals have it from here in. You feel like driving?"

"Sure."

Billings pointed to another news van turning into the parking lot off Market Street. "You see this?"

"Doesn't surprise me. Somebody in New York is watching this with a smile."

"More like a dozen or so are smiling over this in New York," Billings said.

Half an hour later they were on Interstate 95 South heading for Logan Airport in Boston. Billings tried to take a nap, but the young agent was talkative.

"It's only a matter of time before somebody cashes it in on a deal," Callahan said.

"Unless they hired outside."

"They still do that?"

"Smart ones do."

"Still, once that guy goes down, only stands to reason. Nobody takes the rap anymore."

Billings yawned into a fist. "You were local before the Bureau, right?"

"Same crap there," Callahan said. "They wind up in Cedar Junction, somebody gave them up."

"Used to be Walpole," Billings said. "Cedar Junction makes it sound like a resort."

"I heard it was worse back then, the Walpole days."

"It's what they deserved, the shits."

They drove in silence a few miles before Billings gave up trying to nap and said, "Some shmuck probably thought he caught a small windfall to take a guy to Star Island. It's the boat's owner, he had a family, his wife and kids probably wish they never heard of fishing. We ever catch him, the guy did it, he'll cut a deal too. Scumbags. Was up to me, the deals'd go out the window. We're just lazy now is what we are. Waiting on scum to make deals. Pisses me off what happens to the innocent bastards in all this, the guy piloted the killer out to Star. I could care less about Dominick Farese. Fuck him. It's the guy onna boat I feel for. Him and his family."

Callahan's cell phone rang. He answered it while driving. Billings waited for him to finish with the call.

"Right, thanks," Callahan said into his phone.

"What?" Billings said.

"Harbormaster got a name. Was the owner, a Jules Manchard. Lobster fisherman. Thirty-six years old, married, four kids. They're informing the wife now."

"Fuck."

"There's another body," Callahan said. "Gino Malvessi. One of Cirelli's people. They'll fill us in when we get to New York."

Billings opened his eyes. "They played it extra safe," he said. "They hit the hit man."

"They found him behind a bathroom outhouse on the dock back in Rye Harbor. There's a rental out of New York there too, but it sounds more desperate than careful."

Billings wasn't listening. He said, "Sometimes I'd like to skip the bullshit investigations and put these bastards down. We shouldn't waste our time chasing these guys anymore. We should just kill them."

"Huh?" Callahan said. He turned to Billings and saw he was staring. "What?"

"Nothing," Billings said. He looked back out the window at the passing landscape. "Nothing."

■ ■ ■

Brooklyn, New York

Quinlan King put on his earphones and listened to Motown while ogling lingerie models on the Victoria Secret website. So far he liked the blonde models best, although there was a redhead in a matching red lace bra and bikini that had given him a tingle or two. It had become his pastime of late, surfing the internet for thrills. The porn sites were a turnoff. He couldn't get used to all the interracial scenes, Mandingos screwing white women. Those turned his stomach. It was bad enough having to watch them, but then the women begged for their big black cocks.

At least with the Victoria Secret models, he could make up his own fantasies, and it had nothing to do with black guys screwing white women.

Today he was hoping to hear from someone with the Cirelli crew. They still owed him and he was getting anxious waiting. There was the chance they did away with the guy and weren't going to make it public. Then there was nothing he could do about the other half of the money, except it made no sense for them to lose the body. The only point in killing Dominick Farese was to make it public, to show anyone else thinking about making a deal what might happen someday.

King clicked on the link for the next few pages until he found one featuring garter belts and thongs. He felt another tingle in his crotch and started to open his pants when his cell phone vibrated.

"Fuck," he said, then answered. "What? What? What?"

"There was a murder here," his wife said.

King pumped a fist and mouthed "Yes!"

"Quinlan?" his wife said.

"Yeah, so?" King said.

"It's all over the news."

"And?"

"Honestly, I can't believe you."

"You're the one called me."

"I'm getting off the island."

"You said you were taking the train."

"I am. I'm not leaving yet, just getting off the island. There's too much going on there. We're going to stay in Portsmouth the rest of the week. We'll take the ferry to Star Island on the days we have classes."

"Who's we?" King said, not that he cared much.

"Oh, Grace and I. We met in one of the crafts classes. She's a lovely woman. From Ireland. Very thick accent, though. Sometimes I have to ask her—"

"Yeah, she's lovely, I'm sure," King said. He was rolling his eyes, thinking, "Who gives a flying fuck where she's from or what she sounds like, or what the fuck either of you two morons do?"

"So?" he said.

There was a pause on the line. King pictured his wife turning red.

"Hello?" he finally said.

"It's the man you took a picture of," she said.

"Excuse me?"

"The man who was killed. It's the man you took a picture of."

King's eyebrows furrowed. "The fuck you talking about?"

"You used my camera."

"You're nuts."

"Then why do I have his picture?"

King suddenly remembered his cell phone losing power after taking two pictures of Dominick Farese. He'd taken his wife's iPhone and used it to take the next few pictures.

"Quinlan?"

"Huh? What? I don't know. For Christ sakes, what's the difference? I took a picture of a guy. I took a picture of a couple girls, too. One of the buildings there, the water. You have those?"

"No."

"So?"

"Do you?"

"What?"

"The news said he was a member of a New York crime family."

"Who was?"

"The man in the picture, Quinlan. Don't treat me like a moron."

"You're starting to sound like one. Unless you're accusing me of something you don't know a fucking thing about."

"I just hope to hell this has nothing to do with you."

"Goodbye, Mary."

"Quinlan—"

King killed the call, cursed under his breath, then couldn't hold it in and cursed out loud.

Then he began to sweat.

Connecticut

He was driving through Connecticut when he thought to call Doc and make sure he was safe. Doc's sister-in-law answered. She was upset and had obviously been crying. She told him how Doc had been shot outside the Dunkin' Donuts on Arthur Kill Avenue and was still in an intensive care unit at a Staten Island hospital. He'd been hit with three shots, but had managed to kill one of the two assailants. Tommy was guessing Doc had used the compact Smith & Wesson M&P 9mm he carried in an ankle strap.

"He shot the son-of-a-bitch through the eye," Doc's sister-in-law said.

Assuming the line was tapped and that she might say too much, Tommy said he'd call back.

Then he was grinding his teeth and had to restrain himself from driving too fast. It was the biggest downside in working for the mob, no matter the money. There came a point at which they deemed your services no longer required or too much a risk, and then you were dead. Outside of his friendship with Doc, Tommy didn't know the Cirelli people. He'd met the big cheese because it was Frank Cirelli who had the most to lose, the way Tommy had figured it. There was no way any knowledge about a hit on a federal witness could be trusted with subordinates. Tommy had taken the job because Doc had called him, but he'd never liked working for the mob, not in New York, Philadelphia, Atlantic City, or anyplace else. They paid well, but then there was the bullshit you had to deal with; egos the size of whales and attitudes to match. It's what he had to deal with in the past, except this time it was different.

Tommy had read Frank Cirelli wrong and placed too high a value on his own reputation as a hitman. Cirelli had dodged the insult fest that was usually aimed the other way, and Tommy enjoyed giving the wiseguy shit about using an Irishman instead of one of his own. The nonsense wiseguys put a guy through because they felt they could wasn't there the night Tommy met with Frank Cirelli. Tommy had thrown insults the other way, assuming Cirelli needed Tommy more than Tommy needed the money. There's no doubt it was why the price on Dominick Farese was so high.

Now it was obvious Cirelli had played them. All the time the mob boss was eating crow, it was because he had made plans to kill both Doc and Tommy.

Tommy wished he could call the prick now and remind him of how useless his own people were. Not only did they miss killing Tommy, but they'd missed killing a sixty-three-year-old man. So far the score was two dumbski wiseguys dead, and one on the run.

Tommy hoped Doc survived his wounds, but whether he did or not, he was going to make Frank Cirelli pay for the betrayal. The big cheese might be running a crime family, but he was also one dead motherfucker.

He had gone through what had happened over and over to figure out how Cirelli's people knew where he'd be. There was no way Doc had betrayed him, not in a billion years. It was obvious they had someone waiting for him in New Hampshire, probably the entire time Tommy was driving north. Either the guy they sent was from up there around Boston, or he'd flown up from New York. Either way, Tommy had let his guard down, and the unlucky bastard he'd paid one thousand dollars for the lift to Star Island was dead.

Cirelli's guy must have been waiting in the parking lot for the lobster boat to return. What Cirelli's guy hadn't counted on was Tommy getting off the boat before it docked in its birth. He'd instructed the fisherman to leave him off at another dock, and to wait while Tommy hid from his suspicious wife, the bullshit story he'd given the fisherman in the first place. Then Tommy used a Port-O-San outhouse midway between the two docks to change wigs and his shirt. He was on his way out of the outhouse when he spotted the stocky man approaching the lobsterman. The guy probably thought he was about to sell a couple of the lobsters he had on ice when he was shot in the chest. Tommy watched the killer drag the dead man inside the cabin. Then the shooter searched the boat and was starting to look nervous when he gave up and untied the boat from its mooring. He pushed the boat away from the dock and watched it drift a few seconds before turning around to search the area around where he stood. Tommy stepped back inside the bathroom, screwed the suppressor back on his Sig Sauer 1911 Ultra Compact, and waited for Cirelli's guy to get within ten feet before stepping out of the bathroom and emptying half the clip. He pulled the body behind the outhouse and covered it with a piece of loose plywood.

There was little activity on the dock when he dragged the dead man behind the outhouse, but there was no doubt he'd been seen by a few fishermen having coffee near the parking lot when he drove past them. He doubted they knew what had just happened, or that they noticed his license plate was from Connecticut, but changing the plate was the first thing he did once he entered Massachusetts and found a rest stop.

Tommy decided to drive straight through to Baltimore and retrieve a small stash of weapons along with the bulk of his hidden money. He'd return to New York afterward, but there was no way he could visit Doc while Cirelli's people and/or the police were watching the hospital. He'd have to meet up with Alysha at her college and explain why he was handing off so much money for her and her sisters. He'd have to explain how she should hide it and why it couldn't be touched except to pay for college. He'd have to lie through his teeth again for her to accept the money, but there was no way he could tell her the truth, not if he wanted her to keep it.

Then he'd find Frank Cirelli and kill him.

■ ■ ■

Queens, New York

Vito Calabrese still couldn't believe how everything had turned to shit so fast. They were parked no more than 20 feet behind James Doc Adamo's car on Armstrong Avenue when they spotted the old man. They'd been told Adamo picked up donuts on his way to visit a friend in a Staten Island nursing home every Tuesday and Friday afternoon. It was a Tuesday and there Adamo was, carrying a box of Dunkin Donuts as he crossed the avenue, except when Calabrese started the car and was about to pull away from the curb, Phil Avito stopped him.

"No," Avito said, "wait'll he gets inside the car."

"Why?" Calabrese said. "He's right there."

"He's in the car he can't react," Avito said. "Let him get comfortable, sit behind the wheel, and then we do it."

Calabrese didn't see the point. He wanted out of there as fast as possible, but Avito was the one in charge.

They watched as the old man set the box of donuts on the roof of his car before using his remote to unlock the door.

Then Avito changed his mind. "This is even better," he said. "Go!"

Calabrese put the car in drive and raced up alongside Adamo, but the screech of hitting the brakes too hard must have alerted the old man. Avito fired three shots. Calabrese could see at least two had found their mark, but then Adamo raised his arm toward the car and there was another shot. A split second later, red gunk sprayed out from the back of Phil Avito's head. Calabrese shrieked at first, then cursed under his breath and hit the gas pedal. He ran the light at the corner with Avito's body splayed out across the console. Calabrese shoved the body off the console as he turned onto Arthur Kill Road.

Ten minutes later, after heading east at every opportunity, Calabrese was on South Beach. He pulled to the side of Father Capadanno Boulevard and rolled Avito's body out of the car. He nearly spewed when he saw the bullet hole in Avito's left eye.

Ten minutes later, he crossed the Verrazano-Narrows Bridge and was in Brooklyn. He took the ramp for the Belt Parkway and headed west toward Kennedy Airport. Calabrese understood that he had just a few hours before the Cirelli crew would be looking for him. The Cirelli people would never take the chance on him cutting a deal with the law. A botched hit was a death sentence.

On the other hand, a deal with law enforcement was a definite option, but only as a last resort. If there was a way to get out of New York and avoid jail time, Calabrese would take the shot.

In the meantime, he needed money to make an escape. He tried to explain it to his sister-in-law, feeding her a bullshit story about losing a big bet, but there was no talking to the self-righteous bitch. He knew his wife was at her sister's house since she'd left him two weeks ago, the day after she confronted him with pictures of himself and his girlfriend in Atlantic City. His sister-in-law, the bitch, had hired a private detective who had provided dozens of pictures of Calabrese and his girlfriend at night clubs, restaurants, and at the Tropicana in Atlantic City. It was the third time he'd been caught, except in the past he'd been able to deny the accusations because there weren't any pictures.

He'd left the stolen car he used in the botched hit on a Brooklyn street and took a local car service to a motel near Kennedy Airport. He was without transportation and was already low on cash. Watching the local news, he saw where he'd been lucky to get off Staten Island before protest marchers blocked a portion of the Staten Island Expressway.

Now he was desperate and didn't have time to argue. He needed his wife's help, but her sister wasn't giving an inch when he tried calling again.

"No way, Vito," she said. "It's all over the news. There's some kind of mob war going on. Go to your girlfriend and leave my sister alone."

He started to curse when his sister-in-law killed the call.

"Fucking cunt!" he yelled.

He thought about the cash he'd left his wife in a basement safe back at their house, just over ten grand, but there was no way he could go there. She also had one of two keys to a safe deposit box with another twenty-five thousand dollars, some gold coins, and stolen diamonds. He had the other key, but had left it in his night table at the house. If he could get his wife to at least get him some of the money from the safe deposit box in the morning when the bank opened, he could take a flight somewhere. Unless he'd been identified at the scene of the shooting, getting his wife to the bank would be the safest move. He tried calling his sister-in-law one more time, but the line was busy, probably off the hook.

The woman he'd been caught with by the private investigator was a dancer at Lou Testa's club in Brooklyn. She was a looker from somewhere upstate, a tight-bodied, full-chested, brunette, with big eyes and full lips. Vito had noticed her dancing at the club one night and later checked with Testa to make sure she was available. He had been seeing her the last six months, occasionally promising he'd leave his wife someday and never meaning it.

Her name was Lorraine Buchenwald. She danced under the name of Misty. She was twenty-five years old and divorced from a high school boyfriend she'd married after he made her pregnant. She'd given birth to a boy, and then left it for adoption. She moved to New York City a few months later to live with an aunt on her mother's side. She claimed she'd tried working legitimate jobs as an office temporary, but when someone told her about the easy money to be made dancing, she found her way to Testa's club. Since then she'd taken her own apartment close to the club.

For now she was Calabrese's only shot at getting some money and escaping. He'd probably have to take her along, at least to get away from the city, but that'd be easy enough. He'd tell her whatever she wanted to hear. After the botched hit on Staten Island, Calabrese needed to expedite an escape.

He dialed his girlfriend's cellphone and woke her.

■ ■ ■

Staten Island, New York

Frank Cirelli was watching CNN on the small television he'd brought outside while he barbecued sausage in his back yard. He was waiting for the return to a breaking news story about an apparent series of murders in New Hampshire. The last report before the commercial break mentioned a man found dead on an environmental island off the New Hampshire coast. An overhead shot of a beached lobster boat was looped in the background.

Frank cursed under his breath.

It was his youngest son's fourteenth birthday. Except for one of his brothers, most of the Cirelli family had gathered at his home earlier in the week for the Labor Day weekend. So far, except for the birthday, with all the fuck-ups going on around him, the annual family gathering had become a disaster. Frank expected to hear more about it from his father once the old man woke from his wine induced nap. Gasper would give him shit from the moment he learned about the botched work through the rest of the day.

One of two morons sent to whack a sixty-three year old man had been killed, the other was on the lam somewhere, and Doc Adamo was still alive in a Staten Island hospital.

Then there was the moron they sent to kill the Irishman who wound up dead himself.

The fuck else could go wrong was all Frank could think about until his sister removed the top of her bikini and dove into the in-ground pool.

"Jesus fuck!" Frank yelled to his wife. "Get her out of there before he wakes up."

The kids in the pool were all giggling. Frank yelled at them to turn around and shut up.

He'd been worried about what was going on in New Hampshire from the time they flew Gino Malvessi up to Boston. Usually reliable, Malvessi must've tipped his hat too soon. Or maybe he was drinking or flying on cocaine. What was the difference now that everything was fucked?

La Cosa Nostra had been falling apart for two decades. Frank was thinking maybe it was time for the Cirellis' role in the criminal organization to end once and for all. He'd prefer to leave the life on his own terms, but he also understood that nothing like that could happen as long as his father was alive. The old man was still married to the antiquity of *Cosa Nostra*.

At the least, Frank could try and keep his own boys out of the family business. It wouldn't be easy. All three of his sons understood the power of their family name. His oldest had managed to avoid the lure of a street life and was finishing his last year of college. His middle son was a sports fanatic, but had recently started to skip his high school classes. His youngest, the birthday boy, was the wildest, always in trouble in school and recently diagnosed with ADD.

Frank had no doubt what he'd do if confronted with a life in prison. Only suckers stood up these days, but until he was sure of his fate, he would do what he could to maintain what his father had built. He was waiting for his man on the inside of an organized crime squad to call with more information when Lou Testa arrived. Frank watched him pay his respects from outside the insect screen on the opposite end of the pool. He waved Testa over when the big man was done throwing kisses and smiling.

The commercial over, the CNN breaking news story shifted to a correspondent on the New Hampshire dock where two bodies were found.

"You see this?" Frank asked Testa.

"Back at the bar, yeah."

Frank used the remote to kill the television's power. "I don't need this shit now."

Testa told Frank about what he'd heard so far from their guy on the inside of an organized crime task force, that the FBI was scrambling big time because of what happened on Star Island.

"The only good thing that'll come from all this, by the way, what happened to Farese," Frank said. "Everything else'll be up my ass now. We have a clue where the asshole didn't get himself killed by the old man is?"

"Calabrese," Testa said. "No, not yet, but he's been banging one of the broads at the club. He might've run to her for now."

"So there's no confusion about what should happen to him. He should dis-a-fuckin'-pear."

"Of course. Calabrese has me to give up on Adamo. I'll find him."

Frank forked one of the sausages onto a plate he kept on a tray alongside the grill. He cut it in half, grabbed one of the skewers, stabbed half the sausage, and then handed the skewer to Testa. He snagged the other half for himself, took a bite, and spit the piece into a garbage pail.

"What they charge for this shit," he said. "They're the ones should be locked the fuck up, the thieves."

"What about the guy we contracted for New Hampshire?" Testa said.

"Fuck him," Frank said as he turned a ring of sausage on the grill. "He's got half a brain he won't come within a hundred miles of us now, all the attention we're drawing. What I'd like to know is how many fuck-ups we're carrying? We're looking like fucking clowns over here. I'm looking like one. This was a Chinese fuckin' cluster fuck fire drill, Lou. The fuck happened?"

"We sent the wrong people, no doubt about it. Fuckin' Avito. At least he's gone."

Frank sighed. "You take care of Calabrese, get that done without it comes back to haunt us, I'll bump you up."

Testa nodded again. "Done."

"I hope so."

"I'll make it happen, Frank. Like I said, he's got me to serve up on Adamo. Pro'bly more'n that."

"I'm gonna catch a lot of heat from this shit now. One moron gets whacked, the other goes into hiding, and then Malvessi probably whacked some fisherman before he caught it. You made a movie, nobody'd believe it. Not without it's a comedy."

"I know," Testa said. "It's bad." He motioned toward the television. "And now it's national."

Frank pointed to a dish on the tray alongside the grill. "Gimme that," he said.

Testa held out the plate while Cirelli removed the cooked sausage from the grill. Cirelli said, "Ties to organized crime they're saying about the old man we didn't whack. That'll turn into headlines by morning. Then they'll do the organizational chart with my picture at the top."

Testa noticed how his boss stood less than a foot from the grill. "You're not hot standing so close?"

"Huh?"

"Heat from the grill," Testa said. "I can feel it over here, three feet away."

"I need Calabrese to go before he walks into an FBI office, he didn't make a call already."

"I'll head to the club from here."

"Get it done, Lou. Do whatever you gotta' do with this twat he was seeing. Calabrese starts yapping, he gives you up, you'll be tempted do the same thing. No offense, but that's the way we have to think now. Dominoes. The deals they offer, everybody's a tough guy until they're facing twenty years. We don't stop this fast, it'll wind up here, my backyard."

"I'll find him."

"And the other guy in Brooklyn, that arranged yet, the cop?"

"With the kid, Palmieri, yeah," Testa said. "But there's a chance King wrote a note or some shit. Left something for his wife or the newspapers, something happens to him."

"Fuck him," Cirelli said. "He's dead he can't testify. Send somebody with the kid, though. Somebody good this time."

Testa frowned. "Then we have Calabrese all over again, Frank. Another guy has something to sell. Why not let the kid take this solo. Worst that happens, he fucks it up, gets killed himself, or King survives. Who's he gonna tell without he gets inna' shit himself?"

"It's never ending this bullshit," Cirelli said.

He used the fork to turn the sausages again. Testa stood silent and waited. Cirelli motioned over his shoulder toward the pool with a thumb.

"Should'a come earlier," he said. "Missed the show. My drunk sister pulls the top off her bathing suit, dives in."

"She okay?"

"I should be so drunk."

Testa was uncomfortable.

"Alright, look," Cirelli said. "Let the kid do the job. He gets it done, there's no blowback, we'll send him south, put him to work for my brother down Miami until we can bring him back, straighten him out. And if somebody makes him, anything goes wrong … you know."

"Where's your Dad on this?" Testa asked.

"Just get it done," Frank said.

Testa nodded, then exchanged a cheek kiss with Frank. "What about the other guy inna hospital?"

Frank shook his head. "He'll be guarded day and night until he goes home. Leave it for now. He won't talk. He can't. We'll wait him out."

Testa nodded.

Frank pointed to the sausages on the grill as Testa started to walk away. "I'll tell you this much," he said. "I'll never pay fie'dollars a fuckin' pound for this shit again."

Baltimore/New York

The first thing Tommy did when he reached Baltimore was remove his cash from the four safe deposit boxes he'd opened through the years. There were 11 bodies and a few robberies behind most of the three-hundred, fifty-two thousand, six-hundred and fifty-three dollar total. There were also eight ten-ounce gold bars worth up to thirteen grand each as of the last time Tommy checked their value.

The next thing Tommy did was call his daughter at her dorm room in New York. He arranged to meet her later in the day. He was about to go to war with the Cirelli crime family and there would be no skating the consequences. Legally or otherwise, he was close to the end of his run. Taking care of his girls was all that mattered.

He used a burner cell phone to call Doc's home for an update on his friend's condition. He spoke to Doc's sister-in-law again, this time learning that Doc was in recovery, and that a policeman had been stationed outside the hospital room. Tommy assumed Doc's landline was tapped.

"He's got cops guarding him?" Tommy said. "I guess they'll be busy the next few days."

"Excuse me?" the sister-in-law said.

Tommy killed the call. If anything, the police would provide Doc with extra protection.

He spent the next few hours in an apartment safe house he rented in the town of Towson, near the University. He assembled the small cache of weapons secured by his friend Doc over the past few years: handguns, knives and two shotguns, one of which was sawed-off above the handle, his arsenal in case he'd have to go down swinging.

He watched CNN as he packed them in two gym bags, one large, the other small. He brought along four changes of clothing and some toiletries. CNN shifted back and forth from the dock in Rye, New Hampshire, to the helicopter flying over Star Island. The names of the three murder victims had already been released.

CNN assured its viewers that correspondents were on their way to interview the family of the fisherman. An anonymous caller had linked the two men Tommy had killed to organized crime in New York. The FBI refused to comment about an ongoing investigation.

When the news coverage returned to the dock, the reporter said, "And today at least one other killer remains at large. Somebody the FBI and local police believe has probably long since fled the area."

Tommy turned off the television, locked the door behind him, and was on his way. The drive took three hours and fifteen minutes, during which he practiced explaining the money to his daughter. He'd already confessed that it was dirty, but there was no way he'd admit how he'd earned it. He still wasn't sure what he'd say when he called Alysha's cell phone from a parking spot he'd found alongside Washington Square Park.

He kept the conversation short and to the point. She was to come downstairs and meet him right away, no friends allowed. Ten minutes later, he spotted her wearing the orange home Baltimore Orioles jersey he'd given her a year ago. They exchanged a kiss when she sat in the car. Tommy held her face a long moment and smiled.

"What?" Alysha said, struggling to keep from smiling.

"You're beautiful," Tommy said.

"Seriously, Dad, what is it? You sounded nervous on the phone."

"Deliberate," he said. "I sounded deliberate."

"Okay, deliberate. Why?"

He thumbed over his shoulder. "The small bag back there," he said. "It's full of money, for you and your sisters. A few gold bars too. I don't have time to argue about it, so you'll listen to what I say and do as I say. At least this once, okay?"

She was shaking her head. "No," she said. "What's going on?"

Tommy paused a moment before nodding. "I'm going to be leaving for a while, maybe a long while," he said. "The money is what I've put away for you and the twins. You'll put it in a safe deposit box, and never ever give your mother the other key. Either hide the extra key someplace safe, or carry both keys at all times. You use it only when you need it. Whack it in thirds and make sure both your sisters get their share, but you parcel it out. Don't let them take it in one bunch or they might blow it. It's all I can leave the three of you so make it last and make it work for you."

Alysha's eyes began to water. "Where are you going?"

"I can't say. Just do as I say, okay? I'll contact you again as soon as I can, but for now, I need you to listen to me. First thing tomorrow, soon as the banks open, you open a safe deposit box and put the money in it."

"What about Mom?"

"What I just said," Tommy said. "She can never have any of this. I'll talk to her. I couldn't until I turned the money over to you. Now you have it, I'll explain it to her. I'll also tell her not a dime of it is for her. Not ever. Never tell her which bank it is, either. This is for you and your sisters only."

"Are you in trouble?"

"Yes, but it doesn't concern you."

"How can you say that?"

"I'm sorry it has to be like this, but it does, at least for now. Understand?"

"You're putting this all on me now, Dad. I don't know that I can do this."

"I'm sorry, honey, but you have to. The twins are too young and I can't trust your mother. There's nobody else we can trust. Take the money and do what I said."

Alysha leaned into him and sobbed. Tommy held her. The longer they held onto one another, the tighter she hugged him. Finally Tommy pushed himself away and said, "Look, I fucked up, okay? And I'm sorry it's on you now, but I can't help that. I should've been a better father. I know that. I should've been a better man, too, but understand that I've loved you and your sisters more than anything. You have to know that, and you need to let your sisters know. Please, honey."

Alysha cried. Tommy started the car and drove around the park closer to her dorm. He grabbed the bag and walked her to the entrance, hugged and kissed her one last time, then promised to call as soon as he got the chance.

He watched until she was inside the dorm, then wiped his eyes and returned to his car. The trip back to Baltimore would take another three hours. He stopped at an all-night delicatessen on Houston Street for a sandwich and soda. He ate the sandwich in the car, and sipped at the soda as he headed back south to speak to his ex-wife.

Sandi would just blow him off if he called. This time he'd have to get in her face.

■ ■ ■

Brooklyn, New York

Lorraine Buchwald was still wiping sweat from her forehead ten minutes after showering. The lack of ventilation in her studio apartment was stifling. Her rush to pack the things she'd need in such short notice added an extra layer of anxiety to an already stressful day. The phone call from Vito the night before had unnerved her. She wasn't sure what it was about, but getting out of town was something that appealed to her. Maybe Vito really was leaving his wife.

She broke a fingernail trying to unzip an inner compartment in her suitcase and cursed under her breath. She stopped what she was doing to stare at her reflection in the wall mirror across the room. Her underwear were still dry, but the constant back and forth searching for things she'd need, arranging them in the suitcase, then rearranging them, had soaked her t-shirt and left her dripping with sweat again.

"Shit," she said, aloud this time.

She noticed the scratch on her left thigh she'd picked up trying to squeeze past the hamper a few minutes after her shower. Normally she moved the hamper out of the tiny bathroom before showering, but she was in a rush and tried to bypass it without thinking. The sharp edge of the hamper top had caught her mid-thigh and left a six inch scratch that still stung.

Now she went back inside the bathroom to check her weight on the scale she kept under the sink. She was hoping she'd lost at least a few pounds since starting a new diet two weeks ago. Lorraine was a curvaceous 5'4", 120 pounds. She worked out twice a week and was usually careful about her diet. Dancing at the club as Misty four nights a week more than compensated for exercise. Although she was a natural brunette, lately Lorraine was wearing what she'd determined was worth more in tips, a short blonde wig.

The scale read 118. She should be happy, but couldn't now, not after the frantic phone call from Vito. She put the scale behind the toilet bowl and was on her way back to packing when her cell phone rang. Vito had told her not to answer unless she knew it was him calling. She put the phone on speaker and listened to the message.

"Hey, Lorraine, we're in a jam over here today," Tony, the day manager from the club said. "We've got two girls out sick and we need you to come in. Lou authorized time and a half shift pay if you can make it, plus shift choice for the next month. Give us a call when you get this or just come in. We're desperate here, kid. Okay, thanks. See you later."

She finished packing as fast as she could. She was zipping the duffle bag when there was a loud knock on the apartment door. Lorraine jumped at the sound. She thought about not answering. Vito had told her not to tell anybody where she was going or who she was going with, just to get her stuff together, take whatever money she had, and to meet him at a cafe across from Grand Central station. A second knock caused her to gasp. There was no way out of the apartment without answering the door. She looked through the peephole and saw it was the super from the first floor. They spoke through the door.

"Miss, there's water coming from the ceiling in the apartment directly below yours. Can I check your bathroom for a leak?"

"Shit," Lorraine said. "One minute."

She started for the bathroom, then remembered she'd just been in there. "There's no leak," she said. "I was just in there."

The super asked if he could come in and double check. She told him she was indecent and asked if he could come back in twenty minutes or so. She could hear him curse through the door, but then she watched through the peephole as he headed back toward the elevators. She waited until he disappeared inside a stairway door.

Lorraine took one last look around the apartment before leaving. Earlier she'd called a local taxi service for the ride into Manhattan. She was grateful to see the car was waiting for her outside the apartment building. She sat in the back and tried to relax as the cab turned onto Flatbush Avenue toward the Manhattan Bridge. Vito had told her to be there before seven to give them enough time to grab something to eat before boarding the train. She was looking up at the sky as she pictured them sitting side-by-side on the Amtrak ride to Boston. What she never imagined was the black Chevy Impala trailing the cab.

■ ■ ■

Manhattan/Staten Island, New York

Billings and Callahan were briefed over speaker phone by a colleague from the FBI's New York Organized Crime Unit during the drive from LaGuardia Airport to their meeting with the task force at One Police Plaza in Manhattan. A shootout in broad daylight between a known mob associate and two men believed to belong to the Cirelli crime family on Staten Island was being given extra attention. A joint task force with the NYPD organized crime unit was being assembled. Field agents were being reassigned. Billings was assured of total cooperation before he left the meeting.

Out on the street, the sun was setting when he and Callahan stood in Foley Square, a few blocks from one Police Plaza. Callahan asked Billings what he thought.

"About the locals?" Billings said. "Nothing. They hate us interfering. I can't blame them. And we won't depend on them. They've withheld information before. Nothing's changed. I doubt the local units talk to each other. The guys watching the Vignieri crew are in competition with the unit watching Cirelli. That's an NYPD issue, not ours. Whacking Farese stood to benefit both families. I think we're on our own."

"What about our people? We have real support or what?"

Billings chuckled. "Can't wait to get home, huh? Me neither, but our guys are still too caught up in terrorism. Our task forces all over are scaled down, especially in the bigger cities. Definitely here in New York. And every time that happens, resources get pulled from wiseguy details and moved to terrorism or anything else the geniuses running the show deem necessary. And the mob is afforded just enough room to breathe again. Farese was a big win for them, make no mistake. He was in the program. His murder puts a dent in the idea of making deals. Wiseguys start thinking they won't be protected after they flip, they won't be so anxious to make deals. That's all the federal prosecutors care about. God forbid they did an honest day's work, put somebody away without a deal."

Billings pointed to the car they'd been assigned, a black Lincoln Town Car, parked at the curb.

"Where we headed?" Callahan said.

"Staten Island," Billings said. "The old man shot there might be talkative now, although he didn't say a word to NYPD."

"What a life these people live," Callahan said. "What's the point?"

"Point?"

Callahan started the car, waited for Billings to buckle in, then pulled away from the curb.

"Head over to the west side," Billings said. "Guys upstairs said to take the tunnel."

"What's the point of the shit they do to stay out of jail?" Callahan said. "They have to worry about people giving them up, getting killed. They have to live lies, right? Most have families, so don't they give a fuck? This guy we're going to see now, what's his satisfaction for whatever shit he's involved in?"

"This one has an angle," Billings said. "A reason, if you can call it that, but it's not a very good one, not considering who he's working for."

"Who is he?"

"Name's James Adamo," Billings said as they headed east toward the FDR drive. "He's the old man they tried to whack. He's more than rumored to be a rogue gunsmith who provides arms for mobsters. His younger brother was a low level associate involved with the Cirelli crew before he was killed by two of NYPD's finest eight years ago. According to our people here in New York, Adamo held a grudge with the NYPD and decided to help the bad guys."

"They think Adamo helped with New Hampshire?"

"He might've, unless there's another reason the Cirellis wanted to get rid of him. There's something possibly tied to a guy rumored to do hits for the Philly mob. An ex-con tied to one of the few connected guys in Baltimore, also worked with Philly. Name's Tommy Dalton. Our guys in Washington are looking into him. Meantime we'll see if this old man, this Adamo character, is interested in a deal that might let him die with some dignity instead of inside a jail cell."

Traffic on the Brooklyn-Queens Expressway was light, but it still took the agents over an hour to make it to Staten Island University Hospital North. They parked on the street and were surprised to see wild turkeys on the edge of a parking lot.

A few minutes later, a nurse permitted them ten minutes with Adamo. One of two NYPD officers escorted them into the ICU unit. Billings stood at the foot of the bed. Callahan stood off to his left.

"Feds?" Adamo said.

Billings presented his identification.

Adamo made a weak attempt to shrug. "Yeah, so?"

"You won't have this kind of protection much longer," Billings said. "No cops outside your door."

"I didn't ask for it," Adamo said.

"The guy you shot through the eye was with the Cirelli crew."

"Never saw him before."

"Yet you were carrying. Prepared, I'd say."

"It's an old habit."

"Any reason why they'd want to kill you?"

"I assumed I was being robbed."

"Over donuts?"

"Maybe the guy was hungry."

"The guy, the one you managed to kill, he was a made guy, one of Cirelli's crew."

"So, I unmade him."

Callahan smiled.

"I said something funny?" Adamo said.

"It's an odd coincidence," Billings said, "you being shot the day after a witness under federal protection is killed in New Hampshire along with another Cirelli wiseguy."

"Then there's the one you killed," Callahan said.

"New Hampshire," Adamo said. "Where is that?"

"We're wondering you had something to do with it," Billings said. "Because we could replace the locals outside with a U.S. Marshal or two."

"Marshals, huh? Like the wild west?"

"Did you have something to do with New Hampshire?"

"I don't know what you're talking about."

"How about a fella named Tommy Dalton?"

Adamo hesitated a moment. "Who?"

"Cute," Billings said.

"The Cirelli people tried to take out the shooter in New Hampshire and failed," Callahan said.

"And then they tried to take you out," Billings said. "We're not buying the coincidence. NYPD suspects you're in danger. Why you have protection outside. And we know about your younger brother."

"I don't know what to tell you guys," Adamo said.

"You know there's a weapon charge, right?" Callahan said.

"It's registered. Besides, I didn't have that weapon I'm probably dead."

"All it'll take is one guy to spill, Mr. Adamo."

"Like the guy got away," Billings said.

"Spill what?" Adamo said.

Billings said, "That happens, the charges will be federal if you had anything to do with New Hampshire."

"I don't even know where that is," Adamo said. "You guys are giving me a headache."

"An NYPD wire has your name mentioned on tapes going back a few years," Billings said. "They didn't exactly offer it, but it was an old case somebody in our field office knew of when they heard your name on the news. Your name and an attempted mob hit."

"That so?" Adamo said.

"And your brother was around Lou Testa, worked out of his bar for a Sal DeLuca before his demise."

"Fuck you."

"Is that nice?"

"He was murdered by cops, my brother."

"It was deemed self-defense, your brother's shooting."

Adamo said, "Sure, like that Samoan the cops here choked to death last month. Bullshit."

"It's on record, about your brother."

"You know what? I need my rest now."

Billings looked to Callahan.

"He's a tough old bird," Callahan said.

Adamo closed his eyes.

"We'll be back," Billing said.

Adamo kept his eyes closed. "I can't wait," he said.

■ ■ ■

Manhattan, New York

Vito Calabrese was forced to use almost half of the cash he had left to get into the city. Now he stood in the lobby of an office building on the west side of Park Avenue between 41st and 42nd Streets. He spotted the Impala thirty seconds after Lorraine stepped out of the gypsy cab on the northeast corner of 41st Street on Park Avenue. Calabrese and the stripper were to meet at the Pershing Square Café, grab something quick to eat, and then take the seven-fifteen Amtrak to Boston. She was there a few minutes earlier than he expected, but now so was Lou Testa and the latest Cirelli protégé, a punk named Palmieri.

If Phil Avito had done what Calabrese suggested and shot the old bastard while he was crossing the avenue carrying a box of donuts instead of pulling up when he'd already made it to his car, the geezer's hands never would've been free to pull his gun and return fire. Avito was dead for wanting to do it his way, the dumb fuck, but now Calabrese was in the shit because they'd botched a hit and both the law and his own crime family were looking for him.

He had two options: go on the lam, or call the FBI number he'd memorized the day after reading how an underboss with another crime family had kept a similar number on his person at all times.

Calabrese still had a few tapes he'd made of criminal conversations with Lou Testa, including the botched hit, but they were his get-out-of-jail-free cards locked in a safe deposit box on Staten Island. The tapes were his emergency play for the feds. If he could only talk to his wife, she might be more sympathetic than her cunt sister.

For now he needed to know if Lorraine had given him up. She was pulling a small suitcase on rollers and carrying a gym bag by its strap around her right shoulder. If she had the money she claimed she withdrew from the bank, it would be in one of those bags.

Calabrese had little more than a few hundred dollars, what he'd managed to scrounge after the botched hit. He had a single change of clothes, the jewelry he'd worn out of the house two days ago, his cell phone, and the gun he was carrying on Staten Island but never used. If he could get Lorraine to bring him money, he might be able to take off without having to use the tapes. It had nothing to do with being called a snitch and everything to do with maintaining his freedom. Who the fuck wanted to live in Arizona anyway?

He used his cell phone to call Lorraine as soon as she turned the corner. Her phone rang two times before she answered.

"V?" she said.

"Yeah, it's me. Where are you?"

"I'm outside the café right now. You inside?"

"No."

"Where are you?"

"Trying to figure out if you set me up or not?"

"What?"

"You were followed."

"What are you talking about? By who?"

"Testa. He's in a car off the corner. Don't look!"

"Lou?" She said, then started to turn, but stopped. "Tell me you're kidding. What's Lou want?"

"Me. He talk to you today?"

"Not Lou, no. The club called me. They left a message. They wanted me to come in today."

"He was probably outside your building when they called."

"Oh, God, V. I had no idea. What do I do?"

"I have an idea. You're telling me the truth, you didn't bring him here, you'll do what I say."

"How can you even think that, I brought him here? I told you, they left a message for me. It wasn't even Lou who called."

"Then they followed you because they know we've been together."

"I swear on my mother, V. I'd never —"

"Alright, alright. Just listen now. We gotta' do this right so we throw them off. Go inna café, buy something to drink or eat, coffee, whatever, then take the paper bag they give you and put the money you brought in the bag in case they stop to see if you're taking off. Put it in the bag without anybody sees it, then toss the bag in the trash on your way out, there's a garbage can onna corner. Drop it in there and then cross the street into Grand Central. Get on line and buy a ticket for the seven-fifteen to Boston. Lou'll have to get out the car and follow, but he's not gonna head up to Boston so long's you're alone. You take that train and we'll talk later. I'll catch the first train in the morning and meet you in Boston."

"Oh, God, V, I'm so scared right now."

"Don't be. This'll work out, you do what I say. Lou's an animal, but he's missing half his brain. Just do what I say and he'll follow you."

"What if he gets on the train?"

"How's he gonna do that? His car'll be out here. They'll tow it in ten minutes, he's not in it."

"You sure?"

"Positive. Just do what I say and I'll meet you inna' morning. I'll call you tonight to make sure, though."

"Promise you'll call me tonight."

"Of course I'll call. What's wrong with you?"

"Okay. Okay."

"Good girl."

"Okay."

Ten minutes later, the kid from the restaurant switched places with Lou Testa and sat behind the wheel of the Impala. Calabrese watched as Testa followed Lorraine on foot into Grand Central station. Calabrese waited another few minutes before a police car forced the Impala to move. He waited until the car was out of sight before he retrieved the bag with the cash from the trash. He didn't bother counting it until he was safe inside a taxi cab heading downtown, fifteen twenty dollar bills—three hundred dollars.

"What the fuck?" Calabrese said. "What the mother fuck!"

■ ■ ■

The agents were in Billings' hotel room in Manhattan waiting for a fax from the Baltimore office. Callahan stood at the window overlooking 42nd Street. There was a traffic jam on the corner of 42nd Street and Lexington Avenue. An articulated city bus had been hit by a box truck. Horns were blaring. Callahan thought about his home in Concord, New Hampshire. He hated the city and missed his wife and dog.

Billings was watching CNN. A room service tray with the remnants of a late lunch sat on the side of the bed. Four Diet Cokes and a plate of mixed nuts were on a desk with a lamp, a digital clock-radio, some loose change, and hotel stationary.

"This place," Callahan said. "I don't know how people live like this."

"Conditioning," Billings said. "You get used to anything you're in it long enough."

Callahan watched as two men, one in uniform, argued down on the street. "Uh-oh," he said. "Could be a swingout."

There was a knock on the door. Billings looked through the peephole before answering. He opened the door a crack before grabbing the papers being passed to him. He returned to the middle of the room with a fax.

Callahan turned away from the window. "We can go home now?"

"Not quite," Billings said. "Thomas Eugene Dalton is forty-nine years old and has two prior convictions. One when he was a young man, some grocery store robbery he did eight months for before he hit the big time for a botched bank job, for which he served five of an eight year sentence. He's worked for a soda distributor in Baltimore, then as a carpenter with a construction outfit connected to the Philly mob, no doubt a no-show racket. He's been a bar manager-slash-consultant the last six years, during which he's been suspected in at least a few executions for hire, possibly through Adamo. He was believed to be in a car, maybe the driver, there's a question mark there, during the assassination of a New York wiseguy. The hit was believed to be arranged by the Vignieri crime family through a connection with the Philly mob, one Gili Thomasso, a wiseguy operating for Philly out of Baltimore back in two-thousand six. Dalton and Thomasso were tight. He was also a suspect in two other murders not mob related. He has an ex-wife and three kids, all girls, one of which, his oldest, attends NYU."

"That's an expensive degree, NYU," Callahan said. "This Dalton paying?"

"Doesn't say, but what it does say is he was questioned about the murder of the snitch believed to be linked to Adamo's brother's killing by NYPD officers in a shootout."

"The link to the old man."

"Ten years ago. Apparently Adamo is his wife's mother's second cousin."

"That's pretty distant. Think she knows about it?"

"We'll ask her."

Callahan turned to Billings. "We're going to Baltimore now?"

"What? No. We'll call. I'll call. You'll talk to the daughter, see if she knows anything about her old man. He's divorced, he probably isn't talking with the wife anyway. The kid might know something."

"I know of the school, NYU, not where it is."

"I'll get you the address. She's in a dorm there. You can probably take the subway. Meet her outside someplace. Buy her a cup of coffee. I'll be on the phone most of the rest of the day. Maybe there's something else on this Dalton character. Right now, all we have from Baltimore is the word of some retired detective there. He investigated the thing in Annapolis, the one Dalton walked away from. If the old man won't talk, maybe somebody else will. The daughter might."

"Unless she's been coached."

"You'll know that soon enough."

"There a chance in hell we can get back to Massachusetts before the weekend? It's my anniversary Saturday."

"We catch a break, maybe. Otherwise, no way. Trial starts next week, the one Farese was supposed to testify in."

"He's dead, what's the difference?"

"Effect. More windbreakers with FBI across the back, the better the federal prosecutor will feel. That and he'll want to fuck us six ways to Sunday. In some prosecutor's ambitious mind, Farese cost him a future bid at the White House. Keeping us here is one way to make us pay. How many years?"

"Huh?"

"Your anniversary. How long you—"

"Six."

"Kids?"

"None yet, no."

Billings nodded.

"Any word on how they pulled this off?" Callahan said. "Who gave up Farese?"

"They're talking to everybody who was on the island. Could've been anybody. Visitors to the island, somebody works there. Could take months before they have a clue."

"Any chance Adamo would know?"

"I doubt it. Cirelli probably went to him for the shooter. Maybe this Dalton guy, but if they wanted to kill Adamo, he had something to do with New Hampshire."

"When am I going to meet this kid?"

"Sooner the better."

Callahan looked back down at the street. The accident between the bus and the box truck was still blocking traffic, and farther east, in the middle of 42nd Street, a large mass of people were heading west. Callahan squinted to read one of the banners: "I can't breathe."

"What's that?" Billings said.

Callahan sighed. "Nothing," he said. "I just hope it's not far, this school. I can't figure out the subway, I'll be walking."

■ ■ ■

Brooklyn, New York

Luke Palmieri waited impatiently in an Impala on the corner of Surf Avenue and West 21st Street in Coney Island. This chauffeuring wiseguys bullshit was getting old. It was bad enough taking old man Cirelli home to Staten Island a few days a week, the geezer cutting smelly farts every other minute, but today it was Lou Testa and midtown traffic. It was the kind of shit they didn't portray in the mob movies, how making your bones included being a fucking taxi driver.

He watched as Lou Testa spoke on his cell phone across the avenue. All four windows were open, allowing the smell of the ocean to filter Testa's stale cigar smoke out of the car. Palmieri was starving and grateful that he'd parked on this side of the MCU ballpark. If he could smell the franks from Nathan's Famous further up the avenue, he wouldn't be able to resist getting out of the car to eat something.

Palmieri yawned long and loud, hoping Testa might hear him and move his ass. It had already been a long day and he was anxious for some free time of his own. He'd rather return to the strip club they'd started their day at and maybe catch a blowjob from one of the dancers. Anything was better than breathing in Testa's cigar smoke all fucking day. They'd switched driving and riding shotgun a few times, but Testa didn't like opened windows. It was more than a few times when Palmieri had to bring his window down for the sake of breathing.

The worst part of the day was when Testa left him sitting in the car outside Grand Central Station. Testa had followed some stripper on foot, but then the cops told Palmieri to move the car, and he spent the next forty minutes driving in circles so he wouldn't miss Testa when he came back out of Grand Central Station.

Palmieri was getting fed up with the life. He'd been trying to impress wiseguys for two years now. If it wasn't for the few extra bucks being tossed his way of late, he'd been thinking about going rogue and earning his own extra money. With all the abuse you had to take to step up, getting made was no longer considered a prize, never mind an honor.

Palmieri was about to ask Testa if he could leave already, when the big man was finally off his cell phone and waving at him from across Surf Avenue.

Palmieri hustled over.

"I got a job for you," Testa said. "That old fuck gave you shit? That cop? He's all yours, you want it."

"All mine how?"

Testa guided Palmieri into a walk-talk along the Avenue. "Frank wants you should take him out."

"You're kidding."

"This isn't something we joke about."

"Sure," he said. "Be my pleasure, the old prick. Where? When?"

"Half an hour somebody from the bar'll meet you the train station up the Avenue. He'll have what you need. There'll be a car right here after that, keys in the sun visor. Take it home, but don't park where anybody can see you get out. Leave it around the corner, whatever. Pack a bag. You'll head down to Florida afterward. Leave yourself time to get to an airport. You're smart, you'll leave from Newark. Philly, you have the time to drive. Meantime, you go to the old man and do it there, in his house. He left any of that cash around, consider it yours up to twenty K. Anything more'n that comes back to pappa. You do this right, don't fuck it up, it'll go a long way toward your button."

Palmieri nodded.

"You in or out?" Testa said. "We need this done fast. No later than tomorrow noon. You can get to him tonight, that's even better."

"Toward my button, you said, and you gotta ask? Of course I'm in."

"Good. We'll go get a soda for now, give the guy time to get here."

■ ■ ■

Manhattan, New York

"How'd you get my number?" Alysha Dalton said. Hands at her sides, she stood in front of the table where Special Agent Robert Callahan sat. She'd come straight from her dorm room after Callahan had called to request the meeting in a café on LaGuardia Place. It had to do with her father, he'd told her.

"A detective with the Baltimore PD," he said. "He was familiar with your dad. There was a case some years back."

Alysha sat. "Annapolis," she said. "He was cleared of any charges."

"I'm sorry about this," Callahan said.

Alysha waited for more.

Callahan said, "This won't take long. I only have a few questions. I'm more interested in you contacting your father. If you can, I mean."

"Is he okay?"

"I don't know. I'm hoping you can reach out to him."

"He changed his cell number."

"Do you have it?"

"He told me he got rid of it."

"Has he called you? Recently, I mean."

"No."

"Alysha?"

"No."

Callahan waived at a waitress. "Coffee?" he said to Alysha.

"No thanks."

"Water?"

"Nothing, no. Thank you."

The waitress approached the table. "Another coffee?" she asked Callahan.

"Please, thanks," he said.

"Is my father in trouble?" Alysha asked.

Callahan gave it a moment. "Look, I don't know. We think he may have had something to do with a situation in New Hampshire. If we're right, then somebody tried to kill him. We know they tried to kill a friend of his. Do you know James Adamo?"

Alysha shook her head. "No."

"Never met him?"

"Once dad was out of the house, we didn't meet anybody who wasn't already in our circle of friends."

"Mr. Adamo is family," Callahan said. "A distant cousin of your mother's, I believe."

Alysha shook her head. "I don't know him. My mother doesn't really deal with anyone in her family anymore. Not for a long time."

"He can come to us, your father. We can help him."

"What do you mean? Is he in trouble?"

Callahan saw the pain in the young woman's face and shook his head. "I don't know yet. Can you contact him?"

"Why? What's going on?"

"Except for what I told you, we don't know. Honestly. If he contacts us, we can help him. He knows that, but maybe if you tell him, he'll listen."

"He won't listen to me."

"Have you talked to him lately? It's important, Alysha."

"Did my father kill someone?"

"I don't know," Callahan said. "I can't say."

She hesitated a moment, then said, "I saw him last week, a few days ago."

"And?"

"We were in Atlantic City. We met by accident. He doesn't come around much anymore. He stays in touch with me and my sisters, me mostly, but he and my mother don't get along."

Callahan nodded. "And?"

"She told me he's a killer," she said. "A hit man."

Callahan paused a moment. "I don't know that," he said. "Why would she say that to you?"

"Because she hates him. She's not a good person. What did he do in New Hampshire?"

"We're not sure if he was there, but if he was, if it was him up there, we need to talk to him. For his protection."

A long pause ensued. Whatever Tommy Dalton might be, it was obvious his daughter still loved him.

"How do I contact you?" she said.

Callahan handed her a card. "Call me anytime," he said. "For anything, anything at all."

■ ■ ■

Baltimore Highlands, Maryland

The first time Tommy met Sandi was at a strip club in East Baltimore. He was there to pick up shylock money for Gili Thomasso. Sandi was working an afternoon shift, dancing topless to Haddaway's *What is Love*. She was wearing a brown ruffled mini-skirt, brown cowgirl boots with a powder blue design, and a light blue halter she was in the process of removing. Her straight blonde hair reached down to the middle of her back.

"Who's that?" Tommy had asked Joni, a redheaded bartender he'd developed a flirt-for-fun repertoire with since he'd started collecting for Gili.

"New girl," Joni said. "Here about two months. This is her first afternoon. Been working nights mostly."

Gili's money was left in envelopes stored under the drawer of one of two cash registers. Tommy's routine was to sit at the bar, order a shot of Jameson, and wait for the envelope. Some days he didn't touch the drink, but he always left a ten dollar tip.

If he looked at the women dancing on the stage at all, it wasn't for long, except that day he'd looked toward the stage as he approached the bar and liked what he saw.

"She got a name?" he said.

"Susan or Shelly. Something like that."

"She with anybody?"

"Not that I know of. Like I said, this is her first day shift. We work different schedules. I could find out, you want, but then I'll feel hurt, you askin' about another woman with me to stare at."

Tommy set a twenty on the bar. "That's for your pain," he said. "Can you get her to come over before I leave?"

Joni pushed the twenty dollar bill back. She grabbed one of three small flags under the bar and held it up until Sandi acknowledged her with a wave.

"What are the others for?" Tommy said.

"Red's for security and black means it's the law."

Tommy watched Sandi's routine, doing his best to ignore catcalls from the men tossing her their cash. He turned away when one of the men slipped a bill into her G-string after she dropped her miniskirt. When he looked again he saw a few more arms reaching to do the same thing.

"Uh-oh," Joni said.

"Uh-oh, what?" Tommy said.

"You're smitten, Red."

"You think so, huh?"

"I know so," Joni said, "but you better move fast. There's a porn guy's been around here talking to some of the girls. The money they can make for an afternoon shoot's enticing. To some of them anyway."

"Her?"

"I have no idea."

He waited out her routine, and then Sandi made her way to the bar. Tommy smiled as she approached. He saw she had green eyes and freckles, his favorite combination.

"Care for a dance?" she said.

"Right here?" Tommy said.

"Here or the VIP lounge."

"A lap dance?"

She touched his cheek with her right hand. "It's twenty minimum for ten minutes."

Tommy tapped the barstool alongside his. "Sit here a minute, hon."

Sandi looked to Joni. The bartender nodded before moving to the other end of the bar.

"Let me explain," Tommy said. "I say you're beautiful. Really beautiful."

"Thank you," Sandi said.

"My name's Tommy. Friends call me Red. I work for Gili Thomasso. You don't know who he is, ask around. I'd like to date you, take you out someplace. Lunch, dinner, whatever you say. You like me, we'll do it again, maybe a few times."

He stopped to measure her reaction. She was either smiling or smirking, Tommy couldn't tell.

"If it works out," he said, "you like me enough to be with me, then all this shit ends. The dancing, I mean. Only hands touch you after that are these." He held them out for her. "That scares you for any reason, you want to stay in the life, whatever, the money's too good to walk away from, then turn me down now and save us both some time."

"You finished?" Sandi said.

Tommy nodded. "I think so, yeah."

"And if you don't like me?" she said. "There a plan for that?"

Tommy winked at her. "Honey, I can't guarantee much this life, but I can sure in hell guarantee you that much. I'll never not like you, not the way you look."

He pointed to Joni standing mid-bar then. "Even she figured it out and today's the first time I ever laid eyes on you. Smitten, she called it."

They were engaged two months later, a month after Sandi retired from stripping. They married a few months after that, in May of 1993. They had Alysha in '94, and then the twins eleven years later in 2005, a year before Tommy went away for the bank job. It wasn't until he was serving time at the BCDC before Tommy learned that his wife had been on one of the audition lists for the pornographer the bartender had mentioned the night he first met her. Even after their divorce and all the crap she'd dealt him since, including telling their daughter that he was a killer, it still hurt to know Sandi had been willing to give that life a try. He couldn't be sure if she hadn't gone through with it when he was in prison.

Now he was sitting in her kitchen waiting for her. The place was surprisingly neat. Keeping a clean house wasn't one of Sandi's virtues. He thought about taking a look through the house, but stopped himself. There was no point in looking for trouble.

He took in the familiar smell of incense Sandi liked to burn. He remembered her favorites were Patchouli and Strawberry. Sometimes it could be overbearing, especially when Sandi was drunk and lit a few too many sticks at one time, but it had been so long since he'd been around the smell, he didn't mind it.

It was close to midnight. He knew she worked a second shift at a local diner, but he wasn't sure if she'd come straight home or not. Alysha had told him her sisters were staying with Sandi's mother the last few days. Tommy wasn't sure he wanted to know why. Maybe Sandi had a new lover already. Maybe she'd stay out for the night.

He'd let himself in by picking the lock on the back door. He sat up when he heard a car pull into the driveway. He stood up and glanced out the window. It was Sandi, by herself. She was driving what looked like a new BMW. A few minutes later, he heard her footsteps, and then she was inside the kitchen.

"The fuck are you doing here?" Sandi Dalton-Collins said.

She carried several plastic bags by their handles. She set them on the floor and asked him again what the fuck he was doing there.

"Waiting for you," Tommy said.

"You broke in."

"Door was unlocked."

"Bullshit. I always lock the doors."

"I'm here to talk," Tommy said.

"You bring money? Something for the twins, maybe?"

Tommy thumbed over his shoulder toward a kitchen window. "That's a nice car in the driveway," he said. "New?"

"Some cop called me today," Sandi said. "From New York. Kill somebody over there now?"

"The fuck are you talking about?"

"Don't worry, I hung up on him."

"Good. What cop?"

"I said I hung up on him."

"What he want?"

"He asked me about you, if I knew where you were. I didn't bother answering."

Tommy sighed before thumbing toward the window again. "So, it's new or what out there? The Beemer, I mean."

Sandi set her hands on her hips. "I could call the cops here, asshole. Have you arrested for breaking and entering. Don't think I won't, because I will."

He hated to admit it to himself, how good Sandi still looked. She was pushing thirty-nine and looked ten years younger. Three kids, two marriages, two divorces, a few other relationships he didn't care to know about, and she'd held together fine. He even liked the way she cut her hair now, much shorter than the last time he'd seen her, almost two years ago.

"You got an egg timer? You could always use one of those."

"This another Honeymooner reference?"

Tommy smacked the table. Sandi jumped.

"Asshole," she said.

He stood up and pointed a finger at her. "You, are a blabbermouth," he said, a big smile on his face. "That was always one of my favorites, the blabbermouth episode."

"Dickhead."

She moved one of the bags onto the kitchen counter.

Serious again, Tommy said, "Your ex, one of them. He put his hands on my girls?"

"Fuck you," Sandi said. She set her hands on her hips again.

They stared at one another until she gave up and began putting away the groceries. She grabbed the plastic bags two at a time, and set them on the kitchen table. She removed whatever needed refrigeration first, quickly sliding the perishable onto refrigerator shelves. Tommy waited until she was finished with the last items before he offered to help.

"Very funny," she said. "You're a regular riot. How's that for a Honeymooner line?"

"This animosity because you got dumped?" he asked.

"Up yours, Tommy, okay?"

"Hey, it isn't my fault you didn't mention you were married to a felon. Alysha says to me, she says, he was about to run for office or something."

"I'll ask you again what you're doing here, and then I will call the police."

Tommy pointed to his nose. "First thing I noticed, I came in? The smell. Same as when I was still around. The incense, I mean."

Sandi poured herself a glass of Diet Coke from the refrigerator and sat at the far end of the table. She took a sip while staring at him. She set the glass down and huffed.

"So?" she said.

"Even if you believe I'm a killer," Tommy said. "Even if you're right, which you're not, what purpose does it serve telling our daughter something like that? You tell the twins that, too?"

"Look, you've already managed to turn Alysha against me, so I guess it doesn't matter much why I do anything, does it?"

"Turn her against you? Is that what you think? She says to me, she says, 'Mom said you're a killer.' How's that turning her against you?"

"Oh, please, Tommy. Then why'd you flee the city so quick after that other gangster flipped? Why'd you leave Baltimore?"

"You asked me to leave, I'm not mistaken. You're the one told me you'd met somebody while I was inside. The Collins name you hyphenate after Dalton, right?"

"That's none of your business, is it?"

"Where you pick that loser up from anyway?"

"An after hour club, you feel the need to know. Joe worked the sugar plant, nights mostly, but when I met him he'd parlayed the Derby and Preakness into a bigger score than you'd ever brought home. Not that it's any of your fucking business."

Tommy smiled. "Now it makes sense. You were gonna bleed him, a sugar factory worker. He go broke before you had the chance?"

"I swear to God, I will call the cops in two fuckin' seconds, Tommy."

Tommy put up his hands. "Fine, okay. Just tell me this. He the one put his hands on Alysha?"

"She say that?"

"No, but I could tell she didn't want to. Probably because you told her I'm a killer."

Sandi pointed to the door. "You can leave now."

He'd been relaxed sitting in the chair. Now he sat up straight. "How many've you gone through now? I know you lost the prize recently, some lawyer, but blaming me isn't really fair. He found out you were married to an ex-con from some reporter is your fault, not mine."

Sandi glanced at her watch. "You have another minute before I call the police."

"You get anything out of the deal?" Tommy said.

"Yes, actually," Sandi said. "The car was from him. Compensation for the better life I could've given our kids if not for you. I didn't mention anything about you being an ex-con or a murderer, because I never would've gotten the car, would I? You can't see how the kids get the shaft in all this, that's your problem, not mine."

"So you really loved the guy. What else is new? Meantime, your ex, this Collins, he touch my girls or not?"

Sandi glanced at her watch as she sipped more of her soda.

"Fine," Tommy said. "I'll assume that's a yes."

Sandi flipped him the bird.

Tommy said, "Did you even like the guy, you were gonna marry him, this lawyer?"

"What's the difference? He's out of my life now. I'm sure that makes you happy."

"Well, you have that all wrong. You're happy, maybe you're not saying stupid shit to our kids about me being a killer, especially when you don't know your ass from your elbow. But soon's your life turns to shit, or you have to settle for the leftovers from a potential life in the fast lane with some lawyer footing the bill, you take it out on me through the kids. That's some dirty shit, Sandi. I can tell them a few things, too, in case you forgot. Like how I met you, for one thing. Daddy's a killer? Oh, yeah, guess what? Your mother was dancing topless, showing her tits, was about to make a porno the first time I met her. I still don't know you did that or not. We weren't steady yet."

"Fuck you."

"No, fuck you, but you don't have to worry about me saying anything about your past because I'm not that desperate or vindictive. That and I love the girls too much. They don't need to know that shit. Now, what I want to know is more about this cocksucker Collins. He touch my girls, yes or no?"

"Gonna' come to the rescue now, Tommy?"

"It's about the girls, Sandi. I was told he was abusive. I'm wondering if it was just you or the kids he was slap happy with, if it was just his hands or not."

"You really don't think I would've protected the girls if he ever touched one of them? You think I wouldn't have the cops here ten minutes later?"

"I'm their father, Sandi. I'm the one you call."

"So you can come back and kill somebody. Yeah, right. I'm sure the twins'd love to have to explain that at school, how their father came home and killed their stepfather."

"So he did touch them, the prick."

Sandi bit her lower lip, squinted hard at Tommy, then pointed to the back door. "Go."

Tommy stood up. "Fine," he said. "I saw Alysha. I gave her some money and instructions not to give you a dime of it under any circumstances. It's for her and the twins, nobody else. You wanna fuck up their chances at a better life, you go and put your nose in the middle of it."

Sandi stood up. "Get out, asshole. I don't have to deal with your shit anymore."

"Right," Tommy said. He headed for the back door, stopped when he got there, thought about saying something else, something cruel, then decided not to and kept going.

Brooklyn, New York

Quinlan King was packed and ready to go first thing in the morning. He'd set both suitcases in the living room alongside the couch. The call from his wife had unnerved him. If she turned over her cellphone, he was screwed. The FBI would be all over him and there'd be no way to explain why he'd taken pictures of Dominick Farese. He planned on driving south in the morning to wait out the next few days. If nothing happened, he'd return home and work out the details of a quick separation and divorce. If everything turned to shit, at least he'd have some money to flee the country. Soon as the bank opened in the morning, he'd remove the money he'd stashed and take off.

It was a little after one o'clock in the morning when he was thinking he'd like to bite the ass of that Mother of Dragons broad about to take a bath in the hot scalding water. He'd been touching himself through his shorts as he watched the HBO show, *Game of Thrones*. She wasn't perfect by any means, but something about her turned him on. He liked she wasn't shaved, for one thing; too many broads today went for that Brazilian bullshit, made their twats look like they were eleven months old. He'd been enjoying the view until the broad's ass dipped below the water line.

King grew frustrated trying to remember the blonde's other names. Something store bought, or maybe it was storm bought. Something like that. He remembered Khaleesi. That was one of her names for sure. Something, something Targaryon. Daenerys Targaryen, or was it Daenerys Store bought.

"Fuck cares," he said to himself once the scene was over. King found there were a lot of nude broads in just about every episode he'd seen so far. The ass on this one, though, that was something special. He wondered which actors had already plowed her field.

He switched channels when the show ended. He didn't like the one that followed *Game of Thrones*, the one about the broad Vice President, the same broad from the old Seinfeld show. King thought the show was too frantic. It made him nervous, especially all the back and forth insults there was no way went on inside the White House.

"Fuck this," he said.

King fixed himself a gin and tonic while he thought about his wife and how she seemed to settle down once she mentioned moving from that dopey island to some Marriott on the coast. Some hotel in Portsmouth, she'd said they were going to, her and a new girlfriend she'd made on the island. Probably the FBI corralling everybody in a convenient location for interviews, but she was too stupid to figure it out.

King chuckled at the image of his wife tussling with some broad on a bed together. Wouldn't surprise him to learn she'd been a dyke all these years.

He sipped his drink as he sat back down in front of the computer. He couldn't imagine his wife giving him a hard time about a divorce. It wasn't like they had a relationship anymore. He could count the number of times they'd had sex since he'd retired on one hand. It had become adversarial since before he retired eight years ago, but they'd managed to co-exist, sleeping in separate beds the last few years. She'd want to know why now, even though she already knew. She'd want to talk. She'd want to make him hang himself before she agreed to his terms, but she'd eventually agree, he was sure of it.

He spotted one of the brochures he'd picked up about Miami and opened it to a picture of the big hotels and the beach. If everything calmed down, it was the place to go. All that young trim walking around in thong bikinis, their tits and asses hanging out for everyone to see. He wouldn't have to look at some website to get his rocks anymore. He could go for a walk on Collins Avenue, check out all the talent in the flesh.

He started to touch himself again when the doorbell rang. He tried ignoring it at first, but then the thing rang again and again. He forgot himself and answered without looking to see who the fuck it was. That's when he saw the gun, then the wannabe holding it.

"The fuck you supposed to be?" King had said.

The punch hit him high on the forehead, but it caught him off guard. King went reeling backward into the pantry as the punk stepped inside the house and into the next punch. The second punch caught him on the button, breaking King's nose and sending him onto his back in the kitchen. His face went numb. He could feel blood flowing from his nose. Then he felt the flex cuffs around his wrists and he was being pulled by the back of his shirt along the floor into the living room.

"Big mouth, cocksucker," he heard the punk say.

King turned onto his side to keep from choking on the blood flowing from his nose into his mouth.

"This what you do all day, look at broads?" the punk asked.

"It's not here," King managed to say.

The punk spotted the suitcases and smiled. "Planning on taking off, I see. Two suitcases. Nice. You stash the money in them?"

"It's not here," King repeated.

"Ah, nice, gin and tonic," the punk said after he picked up and sniffed the drink. "Very nice. Want some?"

King hugged his arms close to his body and managed to push his shirt up to cover his nose. The punk tossed what was left of the drink at him. King saw the ice cubes on the floor and wished he could hold them against his nose.

"Feel good?" the punk said.

"Fuck you," King said.

"Yeah, right, fuck me. What was it you called me the other day? Guido, right?"

"Asshole."

"Right, that too, an asshole," the punk said. He punched King in the face again, this time knocking him unconscious.

When King woke up again, both his ankles were tied to the dining room table legs with an extension cord. He could hear the punk upstairs. He heard crashing sounds he assumed was the punk going through drawers and closets. He tried sitting up to reach the extension cord, but he was still too groggy. His nose had stopped bleeding, but his shirt was covered with blood.

He saw the highball glass on the edge of his desk and couldn't stop thinking about the gin and tonic, how it was going to be his drink of choice in Florida. He was almost dreaming when he heard the punk's footsteps on the stairway.

"Hey, you're a crafty old bastard. Good spot, the guest room drop ceiling. There's ten K here. The rest downstairs someplace? You have a safe maybe? The fridge? Freezer?"

"Your mother's cunt," King said.

"Is that nice?" the punk said.

King's head was pounding. He closed his eyes tight.

"I'll be right back," the punk said, then kicked King again, this time in the stomach.

It took him a good five minutes to breathe normally again, but he'd already puked on himself. He heard the racket going on in the basement and could only hope the noise was enough for neighbors to notice. He tried to gather enough wind to yell, but it hurt too much to try.

So far the punk hadn't looked in the kitchen or behind the sofa. There was five grand tucked into an opening in the back of the sofa and another five grand in a Cheerios box in one of the kitchen cabinets. The rest was in the safe deposit box at the bank. At least they weren't going to get the bulk of it back.

The punk was back up the stairs and going through the kitchen cabinets now. King wished to hell he would've looked through the window before answering the door. He would have had his own gun in hand and shot the little prick soon as he saw him.

"Okay, you know what?" the punk said. "I don't have time for this right now, but I'll make you a deal. Tell me where you hid the rest and I won't kill you."

King nodded for the punk to come closer.

"What?" the punk said.

King nodded again.

"What, you're gonna say something nasty about my mother again? Remember what happened the last time."

King nodded one more time.

This time the punk moved closer. He stood over King and bent at the waist. "Yeah?" he said. "What?"

King smiled. "Smile, Guido," he said. "You're on Candid Camera."

It was bullshit about a camera, but it was also the last bit of satisfaction King had—the look on the punk's face as the sarcasm and bravado disappeared.

King was still smiling when the punk shot him in the forehead.

■ ■ ■

Manhattan, New York

Special Agent in Charge Billings was about to call and wake his wife when another call was patched through a New York FBI field office. One of the Cirelli crime family had information about the attempted murder of Jimmy Doc Adamo on Staten Island. The informant claimed he was a soldier with the Cirelli family and he was looking for protection. Billings had just settled in for the night in his room in the Marriott at Grand Central when his cellphone rang.

"I have conditions," Vito Calabrese said.

"It doesn't work that way, Mr. Calabrese," Billings said. "Prosecutors and judges are the ones who get to decide conditions."

"Look, I already looked this shit up, so don't try and jerk my chain," Calabrese said. "You aren't arresting me and offering me a deal. I'm coming in on my own. I make the conditions. Either you agree to them or I go away."

"You're looking to make a deal, it means you're afraid for your life. You want to take your chances on the outside, that's your business. The Bureau won't twist your arm. You want to come in and talk, we're here for you, but there's no way you get to make demands before we know what or who you're offering."

It had been a frustrating job so far. The trip to New York, the visit with Adamo at the hospital, putting up with that bullshit, and now knowing the guy he was talking to would get a deal did nothing to soothe Billings' nerves. He missed being home. It was bad enough he was about to wake his wife at one o'clock in the morning. He wished to hell he was already retired. He wished to hell he could shoot the son-of-a-bitch making demands over a phone line.

"I already told one guy what it's about," Calabrese said. "I'll assume he told you before connecting us. The hit on Staten Island, plus a bonus I didn't mention to the other guy."

"The botched hit," Billings said. "Mr. Adamo is still alive."

"Yeah, so how about the guy ordered it?" Calabrese said. "Lou Testa. That enough so you cut the bullshit?"

"And New Hampshire? Know anything about that?"

"Maybe."

"Maybe won't work."

"Not until I have what I want."

"Well, just so you know, before you're given a deal, a federal prosecutor will demand you talk before you get dick. Just so you know."

"Yeah, right. Whatever you say, Mack."

Billings smiled on his end of the call. "Okay, so what about Lou Testa?"

"Yeah, right," Calabrese said. "First you guys commit, in writing, and then we'll talk."

"My guess is Frank Cirelli already guessed what you're looking to do, Mr. Calabrese. You're obviously being hunted already?"

"I have more than a botched hit I can deliver," Calabrese said. "Now, you don't want to talk about what I want, my conditions, maybe you can put somebody else on the line, maybe the federal prosecutor, so's neither of us waste any more time."

Billings rolled his eyes. "You really did do your homework for an escape plan," he said.

"Me and every other wiseguy onna street, buddy."

"La Cosa Chickenshits, right," Billings said.

"Whatever makes you feel better," Calabrese said. "In the meantime, you can hear my conditions or put me through to somebody with clout."

Billings told Calabrese to hold while he fetched a pen and paper. He wrote down each demand without comment. When he was through, Calabrese said he'd meet with them soon as he retained a lawyer.

"You might not need one," Billings said.

"Yeah, right," Calabrese said. "You for real, buddy, or the guy they send out for sandwiches?"

Billings bit his lower lip, then stared at himself in the mirror and didn't like what he saw; an agent of the law having to swallow shit yet again. Instead of calling his wife, he used his laptop to find the address and telephone number of a Staten Island bar believed to be one of Frank Cirelli's hangouts. He jotted down the phone number, grabbed his wallet and some change from the night table, and headed out.

Billings could walk in any direction to search for a pay phone or bar to make the call from, but he was concerned about all the protests going on in the city. There wasn't one now, not that he could see or hear on Lexington Avenue and 42nd Street, but why risk being caught on some security camera along the main drags? He knew the protestors had tied up Times Square earlier in the evening. There was no way he was heading west.

Billings turned left on Lexington Avenue and headed a few blocks north before turning east. Halfway between Second and First Avenues, he realized he was heading toward the United Nations and turned back. He turned right on Second Avenue and walked several more blocks north before turning east again to First Avenue. There he spotted a rare payphone half a block south of where he was standing.

As he headed toward the phone, he noticed there was police activity a few blocks south. Billings assumed the police were dealing with die hard protesters as he picked up a phone and dialed the bar on Staten Island.

■ ■ ■

New Jersey/New York

Tommy drove to New York with the windows open, taking in the smell of freshly cut grass along the New Jersey turnpike. At Exit 4, an NJDOC bus was parked along the road. Inmates in orange DOC jumpsuits picked up refuse along the road. Two guards stood watch.

He'd never been on a road gang. Tommy's years inside were spent with a few Italians from Philadelphia, D.C. and Baltimore. He was protected because of Gili Thomasso and assigned work inside the kitchen, a solid prison perk. If he had to go back now, he'd prefer the road crews. Picking up refuse from the side of the highways wasn't so bad. At least you were outside.

Now he wondered if Sandi had already called their daughter to pump her about the money. He'd considered not telling Sandi, but thought better of it. God forbid something happened to Alysha, both her sisters might go to their mother with the key to the safe deposit box. Though Sandi might turn her war with him into one with their daughter over the money, Tommy had faith in Alysha's ability to keep the money out of her mother's reach.

There was satisfaction in knowing he'd done the right thing. He hadn't been the best father to his girls, but Tommy had always provided for them. Sooner or later they'd know the truth about him, and there was nothing he could do about it. Whether he survived the immediate future or not, chances were he'd never see them again.

He reached Jersey City at rush hour. Frustrated by the constant stop and go, bumper to bumper traffic, he pulled into a diner parking lot. He grabbed a *Star-Ledger* and skimmed the news while he ate a breakfast of steak and eggs with hash browns and toast. Tommy skimmed a few articles before settling on one about the mugging of an Asian diplomat and his chauffer near the United Nations. UN Security cameras along First Avenue were being checked for possible leads. The thieves, two men wearing masks, robbed the diplomat and his driver of cash, credit cards and jewelry. The diplomat claimed his watch was worth more than $40,000.

"I'll bet it was," Tommy said.

When he finished eating, Tommy called his daughter's cell phone. There was one last thing he needed to know, just in case he had the time to take care of it. He was hoping she'd answer and was grateful when she did.

"Dad?"

"Yeah, baby."

"Where are you?"

"Out of town."

"Where out of town? I need to see you."

"Something wrong?"

"I need to know if you're a killer or not."

Tommy cringed on his end of the line. "I told you I'm done answering that question. You're my daughter and I love you. I love your sisters just the same. Everything else is none of your business."

"Daddy, the po—"

"Did you put—"

They'd both spoken at the same time. Alysha yielded to her father.

"Did you put the money away?"

"Yes."

"Good."

"Are you alright?"

"Yes, but your mother told me about your stepfather, that guy Collins. She told me what he did."

Alysha paused long enough for Tommy to know his gamble had worked.
"What did she say?" Alysha said.
"I want to hear it from you," Tommy said. "Unless there's more you're hiding, you and your mother."
"I handled it myself," Alysha said.
Tommy's teeth clenched. "And?"
"He tried, okay," she said. "Just once. He was drunk. I slapped his face."
"Motherfucker," Tommy said through clenched teeth.
"Nothing happened. He tried to grab me one night and I slapped his face. He grabbed my arm, that's all."
Tommy waited for more.
"I told Mom when she came home," Alysha said. "She saw he was drunk and she threw him out. She packed all his shit and left it in the driveway. He left and that was the end of it."
Tommy couldn't stop himself from asking about her sisters.
"No, I asked. And we never saw him again. Mom had to deal with him and the lawyers but not us. That was it."
Tommy didn't believe her. He couldn't.
"Are you going to kill him now?" Alysha said.
Tommy didn't answer.
"An FBI agent came to see me," she said. "He said you need to talk to them."
"When was this?"
"Yesterday. Last night. He said—"
"Where?"
"We met at a café. He said he needed you to call him."
"Your mother call them?"
"What? No. I don't know. He wanted me to contact you. He said you need to call him. You need to go to them for protection. I asked him if you were alright, but he said he didn't know."
Tommy waited for more.
"He said you were in danger," Alysha said.
"I'm not."
"He said you were."
"I'm not."
"I asked him if you were a killer."
"I have to go now, baby."
"Daddy, no."

"I love you. I love your sisters."

"Daddy!"

He kissed her through the phone before killing the call.

Ten minutes later he was on his way through the Holland Tunnel. He checked the GPS once he was in Manhattan. It directed him to another tunnel that would lead into Brooklyn. Earlier in the day Tommy had learned that Doc Adamo would recover. His friend had survived three bullets. Tommy wasn't sure if they'd go after Doc a second time, but so long as the police were keeping watch, there was nothing he could do to help.

He took solace in the fact that the Cirellis had taken their shots and missed. He wasn't about to make the same mistake.

■ ■ ■

Staten Island/Brooklyn, New York

The girl working the bar relayed the message once Frank Cirelli called her back. "Vito Calabrese was making a deal to give up Lou Testa," she said. "That's all the guy said before he hung up."

"When was this?"

"Last night, before I called your service."

"Shit, I didn't check till just now. You tell anyone else?"

"No way."

"You know how to keep things to yourself?"

"Not a problem."

"Okay. I'll be there later."

"I was just about to grab lunch, but I'll wait if you want."

"Do that. Wait."

Cirelli was off the phone and in his car a few minutes later. He stopped at a nearby delicatessen to make a few phone calls and was back in his car. He quadruple checked his mirrors to make sure he wasn't being followed, then made the drive to Coney Island. He found Lou Testa waiting outside a social club on Cropsey Avenue.

"The kid get it done?" he asked, once Testa was in the car.

"Said he did."

"Good. Nothing with the broad, though, huh?"

"Vito never showed. She took a Metro-North train."

"Maybe where he's headed."

"I couldn't follow. Had the car outside."

"Nothing we can do now anyway. He was going to the feds, he's already there. Meantime, I have to see Timkin."

"What's that about?"

"Who knows? Fuckin' bullshit, you ask me. He's probably watching the news and figures we're too busy to pay attention. One of Sal DeLuca's runners caught a beating. DeLuca claims it was Russians did it. He sent a few of his guys to grab one of theirs. It's all nonsense, but I want Timkin to see my face. Yours too. Let them know it isn't amateur night."

Testa chuckled. "Sally sent who?"

"What, you don't think DeLuca knows how to reach out without coming to us? He's running that book a long time now. That moron son-in-law he has at the bar has done a stretch inside. DeLuca feeds him some of his muscle work. Easier he hires his own. Cheaper too. DeLuca knows that."

"Hey, more power to him. I didn't think he had it in him."

Twenty minutes later, Cirelli pulled into an auto shop parking lot on Atlantic Avenue in the Sea Gate section of Coney Island. After being greeted by a pair of Russians inside the garage, Cirelli and Testa were led into the back, then down a flight of stairs. At the bottom of the stairs, Testa was clubbed in the back of the head. He fell to the floor grasping his head. Cirelli was handed a Ruger SR22. He fired three rounds into Testa's chest, then two more into Testa's head.

He left the garage with Victor Timkin, the head of the Russian Mob in Brooklyn. They drove to Lindy Park at the western tip of Seagate, where they finished their business over containers of coffee from a nearby vendor. Cirelli offered Timkin a bonus, one of his bookmaking offices. Timkin assured Cirelli that Lou Testa would be cremated and flushed down a toilet, but Cirelli nixed the offer.

"I need this one to be found," he said. "You can, leave him somewhere on Plum Beach. Stuff a rat in his mouth. It'll go a long way to helping both our causes."

"A rat?"

"Lou was one of my best until he wasn't."

Timkin nodded.

They exchanged a handshake and hug. Five minutes later, driving out of Seagate, Cirelli had to use the visor to block the bright sunlight. He wondered how the sky looked from his brother's condo in Miami and was thinking maybe it was time to head south.

Manhattan/Brooklyn, New York

His cellphone woke Billings a few minutes after eight in the morning. A detective with the NYPD organized crime unit said there was a body at a beach in Brooklyn.

"Lou Testa," the detective said.

"No shit?" Billings said. "He's up there, no? A skipper or something."

"Acting skipper, yes. We're on our way. You want to meet us there, I'll give you the location."

Billings woke Callahan with a phone call and they were on their way twenty minutes later. Callahan filled his boss in on his meeting with Alysha Dalton the night before. Billings didn't seem to be paying attention. They stopped for coffees before heading out of Manhattan. Almost an hour later, still sipping coffees from Dunkin' Donuts cups, Billings and Callahan stood in the Plum Beach parking lot off the Belt Parkway in Brooklyn and watched an NYPD forensic unit remove Big Lou Testa's body from the beach.

"This is starting to look like a purge," Callahan said.

"Cirelli is tying loose ends," Billings said. "Obviously this one had something to do with New Hampshire too."

Callahan sneezed.

"Bless," Billings said.

Callahan sneezed another two times. "The salt water," he said.

They watched as Testa's body was placed in a body bag, dropped onto a stretcher, and then carried back toward a van that was parked near the bathhouse.

Billings turned his back to the beach. "That's the clown the guy onna phone last night was looking to deal away. Vito Calabrese. Had the balls to give me his terms."

Callahan was confused. "One of the guys' shot Adamo? You spoke to him?"

"Call was patched through around midnight. He wanted this, he wanted that, no deal until we agreed, like I can make that happen over a phone. Fuck him. I could make something else happen."

"Excuse me?" Callahan said.

Billings waved the junior agent off.

"What he say, the guy who called?" Callahan said.

"He fucked himself is what he did, now that Testa's dead."

"What?"

"Forget it. Dalton's daughter. You sit on her last night?"

"I told you, for two hours. She never left the dorm once she went back."

"But you think she talked to her father."

"Yeah, she said she did. She was with him in Atlantic City. She knows something, but she's probably too scared to say anything. He is her father."

"Don't go soft, my friend. She's a hit man's daughter, she's not innocent. Probably well aware of how daddy pays her bills."

"Actually, she was asking me if it was true. About him being a hit man. She said her mother told her that."

Billings chuckled. "Fucking people."

"What?" Callahan said. "The kid was concerned."

"I'll bet."

Callahan shook his head. "We leaving this to the locals?"

"For now."

"They know about the call?"

Billings stared at Callahan. "You're full of questions this morning. It's none of their business. Calabrese called selling something RICO, that's federal, that's us. He's running from an attempted hit, it makes sense. Probably Testa gave him the order."

"What time he call you?"

Billings made Callahan wait a long moment, then said, "I already said. He called our New York office. They patched it through to me. Last night, around midnight. He told me he had demands. I told him I needed to know what he had to trade. He gave me attitude and hung up. That's all we have, but we have to assume Cirelli knew Calabrese might look to deal."

"You call a prosecutor?"

"What?" Billings said, his face flushing red.

A thick man in a warmup suit approached them with a badge. He had short, blond, curly hair and wore glasses. "Billings?" he said.

"And you are?"

"Kaprowski," the thick man said. "Call me Ovie. I'm the guy woke you this morning about Testa."

Billings did a double take at Kaprowski, then shook his hand. He motioned at Callahan when he introduced him. "You two'd make the start of a good hockey line, except Agent Callahan doesn't watch the game."

Kaprowski saw that Callahan was confused. "Ovechkin," he said. "Plays for the Caps."

Billings motioned at the van and said, "You expecting this?"

"Not at all," Kaprowski said. "Very surprising, especially the rat was jammed in his mouth. Cirelli sending a message. They don't usually rat until they're charged with something substantial. We don't have anything on Testa. Wasn't charged and he wasn't being pressed. He talking to you?"

Callahan looked to Billings.

"Not that I know of," Billings said. "Maybe it has to do with New Hampshire. Testa, I mean. Or the guy on Staten Island, Adamo."

"Adamo for sure. Calabrese is still on the loose, but he'd go to you before coming to us. Besides, New Hampshire is your jurisdiction."

Callahan was still looking to his boss. Billings glared at him, then turned to Kaprowski.

"We're just down here, detective. Still in the dark as far as the Cirelli people go."

Kaprowski smirked. "Right," he said. "Okay, well, I have to get back." He shot Billings a dirty look and walked away.

Callahan waited until they were back inside their car before asking why Billings didn't mention Calabrese.

"You heard the man," Billings said. "Just like I said, because it's federal. None of it his business. Calabrese said he had more. He'll call back. Asshole shouldn't have hung up on me."

Callahan shook his head again.

"What?" Billings said.

■ ■ ■

One of two people Tommy killed without financial incentive was a lawyer his only sister had once worked for and became involved with. Fiona Dalton was a few years younger than Tommy, somewhat cognitively impaired from oxygen deprivation at birth, and attractive enough for men to pursue her. The runt of the litter, their mother had called her, except the injustice of his sister's situation had always bothered Tommy. It was a big reason why he'd quit believing in the bullshit Catholic mumbo jumbo his parents and older brother seemed to cling to.

On the day Fiona was fired, Tommy was having lunch with Doc Adamo in Baltimore. Tommy learned about the firing from his mother, an emergency call from the hospital where Fiona was recovering from an attempted suicide. It was how the family first learned about Fiona's abortion, in the suicide note she'd left in her bedroom:

Please forgive me, Mom. I can't live without Doug. He made me get an abortion last month and today he fired me. I'm sorry. — F.

Tommy learned from his mother that Fiona had been dating an attorney where she worked as a receptionist. His name was Douglas Benelli and he was married. "It didn't take me but ten minutes to learn he had a wife and two kids," Eleanor Dalton told her son. "But you know how your sister is. Somebody took interest in her looks, like all the rest. He didn't ignore her, you know, her issues, and she fell in love. The shit drives a Maserati on top of it. Probably leases it, the asshole. Big fish in a small pond, and I had to look the other way for her sake, but now he's hurt Fiona to the point she wants to kill herself? It's not right, Tommy."

Tommy was crazed and wanted to kill Douglas Benelli the same night, but Adamo stayed in town an extra few days to try to keep him calm. After three days, Adamo agreed to have a talk with the attorney for what Tommy claimed would be nothing more than financial compensation for his sister. They found Benelli at an upscale Baltimore restaurant the attorney frequented a few days a week.

They waited at the bar inside the restaurant and saw when Benelli pulled up to valet park his blue Maserati. When they saw he was alone, Adamo approached him first.

"Douglas Benelli?" he said.

"Yes," Benelli said, looking from Adamo to Tommy.

"I'm Fiona's brother," Tommy said, cutting Adamo off.

Benelli went to shake his hand but Tommy didn't take it. "I'm sorry to hear what happened," he said.

"How sorry?" Tommy said.

"Excuse me?"

Adamo put a hand on Tommy's chest as he stepped closer to the attorney. "You can understand he's a little upset," he told Benelli. "The family learned about the abortion in Fiona's suicide note."

Benelli was surprised. He immediately raised both hands and stepped back. "I'm sorry, but I can't discuss anything about this right now," he said. "And I don't know anything about an abortion."

"Yeah, well, we didn't think you'd want to talk about it," Adamo said. "We're only here to discuss reparations, counselor."

Benelli's hands were still raised, but this time he smirked. "You're kidding, right?"

Tommy lunged for Benelli, but Adamo managed to restrain him.

Benelli had stepped back. "Hey, I'll have the police here in two minutes," he said. "Back the fuck off."

Tommy was glaring at the attorney. Adamo told Tommy to stay calm.

"What?" Benelli said, suddenly cocky. "Are you trying to threaten me with that stare? Right here in front of an entire restaurant?"

The maitre d' suddenly appeared alongside Benelli. He asked the attorney if he needed the police to be called.

"No need," Adamo said. "He's just upset is all. I'll walk him out."

Adamo ushered Tommy outside. He told him to wait there and stepped back inside. Benelli was returning Tommy's stare through the restaurant front windows. Adamo approached him and said, "Look, I'm gonna say this once. You have no idea what you're dealing with here. What happened between you and Fiona isn't going away. You and I both know she can take you to court. At least think it over and give her mother a call. Make an offer or something."

Benelli was scrunching his face in disgust. "Let me tell you something," he said. "You really think some court is gonna take the word of some retard over mine? Think about it."

Adamo couldn't believe his ears. He shook his head, started to turn away, then stopped and said, "Are you serious?"

"You're fuckin' right I am," Benelli said. "So do yourself a favor and take that idiot outside and get lost, the both of you."

Adamo gave it a moment, then smiled. "Sure," he said. "Fine, no problem."

As soon as he was outside he could see Tommy was still glaring into the restaurant.

"What he say?" Tommy said without moving his eyes from where he was staring.

"Nothing," Adamo said before he leaned in close to Tommy. "We'll kill the prick."

On their way back to his Towson apartment, Tommy insisted on driving his SUV through the valet parking section. Adamo tried to stop him, but to no avail. Tommy sideswiped the Maserati. Adamo insisted on taking the wheel a few minutes later, but then he made a wrong turn and drove them ten miles out of their way. Tommy found it funny and hadn't let Adamo forget it since.

Six weeks later, Adamo returned to Baltimore and joined Tommy in settling the score. Although he would've taken more pleasure in gutting the piece of shit, Doc Adamo had convinced Tommy to use a Browning X-Bolt Stalker 30-30.

"He was cocky, this lawyer," Doc had told Tommy. "Felt he was untouchable, right?"

"Yeah, so?" Tommy said.

"So you put one in his stomach first, so he knows what just happened, wait a few seconds, then kill him with the second shot. You'll get to watch him lose all sense of cockiness. You'll see it that way, the terror in his eyes."

He and Doc had set up a blind from the woods surrounding one end of the parking lot outside the building where Douglas Benelli practiced law. When the lawyer left work for the day, he was walking alongside a young woman. Both were smiling a moment before Tommy squeezed off the first shot and created a small crater in Douglas Benelli's stomach. The lawyer bent at the waist before falling back on his ass. He was clutching his stomach when he finally looked up, the terror Doc spoke of clearly in his eyes. Tommy aimed higher and put the second round through the center of the lawyer's chest as the woman screamed first, then ran and ducked behind the restored Maserati.

Now, after looking over a topographical map of Staten Island, Tommy was thinking he'd kill Frank Cirelli the same way, from a wooded area indicated on the map. According to the Google map, Cirelli's house was directly across the street from the woods. Tommy would have to survey the area before setting up a blind. From what he could tell from the map, there was a decline where the woods began at the road in front of Cirelli's house.

In the meantime, he was eager to perform some collateral damage to the same crime family. The bookmaker who'd gotten Doc's brother killed, Sal DeLuca, was at the top of the list.

He wasn't wearing a wig when he approached the maître d' at Gargiulo's in Coney Island. He slipped him a twenty dollar bill and asked where he could place bets on the first week of action in the NFL.

"What kind of bets you talking about?" the maître d' said.

"Big ones," Tommy said. "I don't like betting with some computer and my guy was recently forced to retire, soon's the preseason ended. So far, all I'm finding is one and two dime maximums, but I was told to ask here."

"I'm not sure you'll get more than two dimes without reliable references, not without putting cash up front."

"Yeah, except I don't know they won't take it to the craps tables Atlantic City. You ask for up front, you make me nervous."

"You're betting more than two dimes a game, they'll want to make sure you're not looking to rape them, especially they don't know you, you're off the street like this."

"How much up front?"

"You'll have to ask Sal, but I'm thinking least half of what you're looking to bet. These guys aren't amateurs."

"Shit, fine then. It's already too close to dick around. I'll put it up. Half the cash."

"You got inside information or something?"

"I did, I'd go to Vegas and use a bank check. Can you help me out or what?"

A couple approached the desk. The maître d' excused himself a minute. He pulled a pen from his shirt pocket and wrote an address on the back of a card before handing it to Tommy.

"Go there, ask for a guy named Sally. But don't waste your time trying to bet the numbers you're talking about on credit. He'll want to see it first, the cash. This guy's no rookie."

"Fair enough," Tommy said. "Thanks."

"Not a problem," the maître d' said. His hand was out.

"You're kidding, right?" Tommy said. He shook the maître d's hand and left the restaurant.

He plugged the address into his GPS when he was back in his car, waited a moment, and saw it was just a few blocks away. Tommy wondered if he should walk instead of trying to find another parking spot, then decided it was best to keep the car close at hand. He started the engine and pulled away from the curb.

Five minutes later he found a spot when a black woman pulled away from the curb half a block from the bar. Tommy noticed the bar door was open when he passed. Either the air conditioning wasn't working or the place was too empty to waste the electricity.

He put on a Phillies baseball cap and pulled the beak down low on his forehead. He brought the Ruger LC9 to conceal underneath his windbreaker. The Heckler & Koch HK45 was the one he'd walk into the bar with, his right hand and the weapon inside the Dunkin Donuts bag he'd shoot through. If the maître d' had called ahead to try and rob him of any cash he might be carrying, they might assume the bag was holding the money. If not, he'd be able to sit at the bar and order a beer before asking for Sally.

First he watched his passenger side mirror for traffic entering or exiting the bar. He waited a full five minutes before getting out of the car. He scanned the street for any street surveillance, then walked past the bar once, taking a quick glance inside the open door. If there was police surveillance on the place, Tommy wasn't seeing it.

There was a fat man with a cell phone to his right ear at the opposite end of the bar when Tommy stepped inside. Steam rose from the cup of coffee in front him. The bartender, a tall thin man with a thick mullet, was cutting limes. Tommy noticed a sign above the bar that read: Ladies Night, Every Night.

Tommy didn't see any ladies. He didn't see any customers either, unless the guy at the end of the bar was on the wagon. He took a seat on the stool and left the bag with the .45mm on the stool alongside him. The place smelled like peanuts, piss and stale beer.

"Can I help you?" the bartender asked.

"I'm looking for Sally."

The bartender pointed at the fat man.

"Thanks," Tommy said. "Let me have a beer in the meantime. Whatever you have on draft."

"I have three different beers on tap," the bartender said.

"Surprise me," Tommy said. He slid a hand inside the bag and was off the stool.

"You the guy from the restaurant?" the fat man said.

Tommy nodded.

The fat man held up a finger. He said something in his cell phone, then set it down on the bar. He slid off the stool.

"You wanna bet cash, I gotta pat you down," the fat man said. He stopped halfway down the bar and opened the men's room door. "After you."

Tommy smiled. "Sure," he said. "No problem."

■ ■ ■

Manhattan, New York

Gasper Cirelli mopped the sauce from the edges of his plate with a piece of semolina Italian bread. He bit off a chunk of the sauce soaked bread, then wiped his mouth with a napkin. He'd just finished a late lunch, *scungili* in a *fra diavolo* sauce. He was waiting for his son to return from an emergency meeting with the underboss of the Vignieri crime family. Gasper had come to the family owned restaurant on Mulberry Street in the morning. He'd taken a long peaceful walk along Christie Street, where he stopped to watch a group of elderly Chinese doing their *tai chi* exercises. Gasper remained fascinated at the slow motion harmony the group maintained.

He smelled incense as he approached Second Avenue. He took in the strawberry scent, then turned and headed back south. The smell of marijuana forced him to cross the street.

"Fuckin' kids," he said to himself.

He was back in the restaurant on Mulberry Street in time to see the breaking news on the television screen over the bar. There'd been a double homicide at a bar in Coney Island. The names of the victims were being withheld until their families were notified, but Gasper suspected one of the two victims was Sal DeLuca.

"Shit," he said.

A few minutes later he ignored a phone call from Ft. Lauderdale, Florida. He recognized the area code, but still wasn't speaking to his youngest son.

Gasper was too preoccupied with genuine concerns about a possible war with the other New York crime families he knew he couldn't win. It had become hard enough having to deal with snitches, but a war would destroy what he'd spent his life building. The news coverage alone would require extra local and federal law enforcement pressure, the last thing *La Cosa Nostra* needed. The other thing that troubled his thoughts was concern for Frank.

He was relieved a few minutes later when his son returned to the restaurant. Gasper moved to a booth. Frank joined him, sitting directly across the table.

"You know about Coney Island?" Gasper said.

Frank nodded. "Wasn't sanctioned. No other crews."

"You sure?"

"Pretty sure, or I wouldn't be here, right?"

"Not funny."

"Wasn't meant to be."

Gasper shook his head. "I don't like it," he said.

"Look, it's not the Vignieris did that at the bar. Nobody else would make the move without them."

"Foreigners?"

Frank shook his head. "No. I'm thinking the other guy. The one I sent up north."

"Shit. We know where he is?"

"I knew that, it've been done already."

Gasper rubbed his face with both hands.

Frank said, "He's coming for me."

"What?"

"It's me he wants. Because we missed. Him and Adamo."

"You sure?"

"Wouldn't you?"

Gasper shrugged. "The Vignieris send Sforza?"

Frank nodded. "Showing muscle with their underboss, yeah."

"What he have to say?"

"Wanted to know what the fuck is going on?"

"He's feeling you out."

"I know, Pop. There's blood and they smell it."

"If they think you're going down—"

"I know Pop. I know."

■ ■ ■

Brooklyn, New York

Detective Kaprowski from the NYPD organized crime unit was already on the scene when Special Agent Callahan arrived. Kaprowski stood inside the entrance to the bar and stopped Callahan from entering, telling him homicide had first crack. Then he asked Callahan about his partner.

"Supervisor in Charge," Callahan said, correcting the detective. "He's back to the city. Something important, I'm sure."

Kaprowski chuckled. "You don't get along with him either, huh?"

Callahan ignored the comment.

"You're young," Kaprowski said. "How long you with the feds?"

"Not long," Callahan said.

"From up there, New Hampshire?"

"Concord."

"Never been," Kaprowski said. "Never been north of Connecticut. PD there?"

"Four years."

They watched as the homicide detectives stepped outside of the bathroom.

"We can take a look soon as they say," Kaprowski said.

"Any video?" Callahan said.

"Nothing inside," Kaprowski said, "we'll check the Citibank up the street. That might have something."

"What are you thinking about all this?" Callahan said.

Kaprowski shrugged. "Could be a war. Could be a purge. If that's the case, you're here for the right reason."

"Farese," Callahan said.

"It's a safe bet. Unless it's a war, but there's nothing to suggest that. At least nothing on our radar. We'll know more in a few days."

"Few days?" Callahan said. "I was hoping a few hours."

Kaprowski smiled. "You know you have a hockey name, right?"

"Clint Eastwood too."

"Shit, I forgot about that. Dirty Harry."

Callahan winked.

"You go to any games? Boston, I mean. Not that I can stand them, the Bruins."

"I'm not really a fan," Callahan said. "I prefer baseball, sometimes. College football. Can't stand the pros, all the celebrating they do after each play."

"Then you'd love hockey," Kaprowski said. "It's totally team oriented. They have their superstars, but they don't mean shit without a team behind them. Nothing like the NBA, and it's just as violent as football, minus the celebrations. They only celebrate after a goal and there's very little chest banging. Even when there is, most guys credit their linemates. You should give it a shot. You might like it."

"Maybe when I get home."

"I used to be a Rangers fan until they traded our captain. The guy with your name. He's with Tampa now. Tampa Bay Lightning. Bolts for short."

Callahan yawned.

Kaprowski smiled. "I'm boring you, huh?"

"Anybody see the shooter?"

"A couple passing by said they saw a man leave the place wearing a red baseball cap. He went up the block and got in a car. They weren't watching after that."

"They give a description?"

"Yeah, except they contradicted one another. One said five-ten or so, thin, wearing light faded blue jeans and sneakers, the husband said he was six-two, stocky and he didn't see what he was wearing except for the cap. Thought it was a Jersey Devils hat. Of course it could've been Reds or Phillies. It was definitely red. Bartender must've got off a round with the shotgun before he bought it."

"Hit anybody?"

Kaprowski pointed at the wall alongside the men's room. "That."

A detective with homicide waved at them. Callahan followed Kaprowski into the men's room. They stepped inside and could see a body sitting upright on the floor, dead from two bullet wounds to the forehead. Nothing had been removed from his person.

"Sal DeLuca," Kaprowski said. "He was a bookmaker with the Cirelli crew forever. Goes way back."

"That make sense?" Callahan said. "A bookie and a bartender?"

"Bartender's more muscle than barkeep. For DeLuca, collections and so on, but no, it doesn't make sense. Bookies aren't the guys get whacked unless they're caught stealing. Like I said, DeLuca's been with Cirelli forever. Bookmakers are accountants to wiseguys, nothing more'n that. He was stealing, I'm sure, but nothing big enough for this. We'd've known. There would've been chatter. We'll know more—"

"In a few more days."

"Look, we have a wire on this place and a few more. Ones operating under Cirelli's umbrella. Word is there was a suspicious call put into a joint on Staten Island the night before we found Testa's body. I haven't heard it yet, but it might be something."

Callahan's brow furrowed. "What time was the call?"

"I'm not sure. Why?"

Callahan frowned. "How long'll that take, listening to the wire from the bar?"

"A day or so, you guys don't request it first." Kaprowski said. He slapped Callahan on the back. "You could always trade in the sunglasses, go back to something respectable."

Callahan nodded. "Thought's crossed my mind," he said. "Then again, police here have their own headaches. How do you stand it, the protests and so on?"

"Couple idiots, what you're talking about. Problems' with the public, they see that shit, nothing happens, they blame all of us. They don't get it, what happens sometimes. Could be a rookie on the force six months, could be a ten year veteran. You're confronted with something split second, you don't have time to guess. The other thing they don't see, the public, the cops helping old lady's up a stairway, giving one of the homeless half their sandwich, protecting some kid from a drunk father is about to beat him half to death. Doesn't make the news, nobody sees it. Nobody uses their cellphones to record that stuff."

"Yeah, but cigarette lighters? Those dollar plastic things they sell in Bodegas and gas stations?"

Kaprowski shrugged. "Like I said, a couple idiots. They ruin it for the rest of us. I'm too invested now to sing or dance."

Callahan nodded, a faint smile showing.

They stepped back out of the bathroom and were led to the end of the bar where the bartender lay face down in a pool of blood. The body was just outside the end of the bar. A sawed-off shotgun lay on the floor a few feet away. He'd been shot in the face once and twice in the chest.

Callahan had seen worse, but not often. A smalltime biker war in Concord resulted in two bodies hacked to death and left in a ravine off Interstate 93. Callahan had just finished eating lunch when he arrived on the scene. He lost his lunch and breakfast when he realized one of the bodies was a pregnant woman, her baby's head visible in an open wound. He doubted anything would ever be that bad again. So far he was right.

Kaprowski's cell phone rang. He answered it while Callahan ran a hand under the length of the bar. If there was a hidden surveillance microphone in the bar, it wasn't under the lip of the bar top. It had happened before, one of two law enforcement agencies keeping secrets from the other. It had happened in Manchester, New Hampshire, the same year he found the hacked bodies, except that time it was the feds who'd kept secrets from the local police.

"It's getting busy," Kaprowski said, off the phone now.

Callahan looked up at him. "What's that?"

"One of ours, organized crime," Kaprowski said. "Retired. Homicide says it looks like a home invasion, maybe a push-in, somebody looking for something. The place was ransacked."

"I'm not following."

"One of our retirees from organized crime," Kaprowski said. "He was killed last night, early this morning. His place was ripped up, someone looking for something."

"You know the guy?"

"No, but my father probably did," Kaprowski said. "My old man started this unit back in the seventies. Quinlan King is the guy was killed. Homicide says he took a beating. He was cuffed and tied."

"Sorry," Callahan said.

Kaprowski nodded. "Here's the kicker. They located the wife. She's been away, some kind of artistic retreat on some island off the coast of —"

"New Hampshire," Callahan said. "Star, more than likely. Holy shit."

"Yeah," Kaprowski said. "Holy shit."

■ ■ ■

The apartment was on the 8th floor of a building facing Jamaica Bay. Calabrese had been sitting on an uncomfortable folding chair in the living room two hours already and nobody was speaking to him about any deals. There was a television on, a Yankees game, but the volume was too low to hear what was being said. So far he'd mostly been ignored by the agents guarding him. He was anxious to use the bathroom. The one sitting in the armchair looked no older than twenty-five. He'd been watching the game, but looked about to doze off. The door buzzer sounded. The agent in the kitchen said something Calabrese couldn't hear into the intercom, then returned to the living room and pointed to the bathroom.

"Go now, you have to go," he said.

Calabrese had to piss with the door open. The sleepy agent stood in the doorway yawning while Calabrese did his business. Calabrese asked if they'd do the same thing if he had to take a shit, but neither agent smiled at his attempt at humor.

A few minutes passed before the apartment door opened and someone brought in food. Calabrese was handed a ham and Swiss sandwich with a tiny container of potato salad and a Diet Coke. He ate and drank in silence while both agents continued watching the game. He wondered if they ever bet games and thought about trying a bookmaking joke. He decided against it when there was a commercial for *Dancing With The Stars*. Some celebrity football player with a hot-looking piece of ass he figured the football player was banging. She reminded Calabrese of Lorraine and how that bitch had cut him loose with just a few hundred dollars.

Another half hour passed before the agents' relief arrived, a single older guy it looked like. The two agents Calabrese had surrendered to left them alone. He sipped at the last of his Diet Coke when the relief agent introduced himself as a Special Agent in Charge.

"In charge of what?" Calabrese said with a smirk.

"Sandwiches," the agent said.

Calabrese lost the smile.

Until then, he was hopeful the old guy was the big shot he'd been waiting for. Now that he realized who he'd just insulted, Calabrese swallowed hard and said, "Look, I can give you a few people. Lou Testa didn't get whacked, I could've given you him."

"That mean you have new conditions?" the agent said.

"I guess I deserve that," Calabrese said. "You're the guy, the other night?"

"Agent Billings, yeah. I'm the one goes out for sandwiches."

Calabrese couldn't believe his run of bad luck. "Sorry," he said.

"I just hope you have something important to say," Billings said. "I've already been to the beach where your buddy washed up. Mr. Testa isn't going to help your cause now. Your boss talks first, you're fucked again. He's the big fish in this, and lately the big shots make deals too. *La Cosa* bullshit some of us call your Mickey Mouse club. He does that, your boss, he flips, he's home free and you're gone for ten minimum on a RICO charge. He doesn't talk, you have a shot, but I wouldn't expect too much unless you have something a federal prosecutor can work with."

"Alright, look," Calabrese said, leaning forward on the folding chair. "I was a little out of line the other night, I admit it. I had my reasons. Testa was out to whack me. Some broad I've been bangin' the last few months, one of the strippers from his club in Brooklyn, we were gonna take off together, head out of town, but then I seen they followed her to where we were meeting and I panicked. I knew I couldn't go home. The wife is pissed at me for having a girlfriend. Her fucking sister put a private dick on me, took pictures. Her sister, that cunt, she hates me more'n cancer. So here I am. Turned myself in.

"The main thing? I don't wanna do time. Not any. I don't care where yous send me, could be cold or hot. I'm pretty sure the wife won't come, but you never know. I won't fight her on the kids, but I'm thinking this is my only out. I wanna die an old man and I don't care where it happens."

Billings said, "You don't have enough to warrant a relocation, Vito, you won't get one. That's the thing you need to understand. It's not what you want."

"Even I clear up a couple hits?"

"Depends, if you were involved, you'll have to do some time for them." Calabrese waved his hand. "No way. Uh-uh."

"Sorry, but yes way," Billings said. "Maybe you need some more time to do the research. Even the guys who gave up bosses had to go away for a few years. Even the bosses. Protective custody, don't get me wrong, but they still went away."

"Shit," Calabrese said.

"I was you, all the backstabbing in your racket, I'd start spewing," Billings said. "Either that or you're free to take a fucking hike. NYPD wants you for the old man, Adamo, but personally, I don't give a shit. You have three choices, come to think of it. You can talk to us, or I can turn you over to New York's finest, or you can wait until I take a piss and walk out the door. I won't stop you. There's probably action on the street right now, an over-under, on how long you survive if you don't flip. So, you want to walk, be my guest."

Calabrese stared at Billings a long moment, then said, "You're enjoying this aren't you?"

Billings winked, said, "More than you know."

Ft. Lauderdale, Florida

Luke Palmieri had taken a flight from Philadelphia to Ft. Lauderdale the same day he killed Quinlan King. He'd booked a room at the Ritz-Carlton with his own credit card before the flight took off from the airport. He had a few cocktails before boarding the flight and was asleep before the jet reached cruising altitude. He woke up just before landing, never having to refasten his seatbelt.

He took a cab from the Ft. Lauderdale airport to the hotel, checked in, recounted the money he'd taken from Quinlan King's home, and then danced in front of the mirror holding onto some of the cash. He showered, shaved, and then headed down to one of the hotel bars to scout the local talent. Luke wasn't disappointed. He saw beautiful women everywhere, most of them scantily dressed because of the high August humidity.

He bought himself a Vodka tonic at the bar, introduced himself to a tall blonde with long legs and a big chest. He was rebuffed when she ignored his hand and turned her back. Then a man who could've been her father suddenly appeared and led the woman away.

"Fuck you, too," Palmieri said under his breath.

He was proud of himself and couldn't resist reminding himself why.

I killed a motherfucker, bitch. Put two in his fat stomach and another one in his fucking head. Bada-boom, bada-bing, I'm months, maybe weeks, maybe days from being a made man. Then I'll come back here and say hello to your blonde girlfriend, wife, daughter, whatever the fuck she is to you, by sticking my hand up her dress, diddling her twat. How's that, pal?

He smiled thinking about his new sense of accomplishment. He was on the cusp of being a made guy, a full-fledged wiseguy. He was on his way to being one of his movie heroes, like Sonny Corleone in *The Godfather*, or Tony Spilotro in *Casino*. He had money, he had looks, he had his youth, and now he was a killer. The world was his.

So fuck these stuck-up Miami bitches.

He finished his drink and walked away without leaving a tip. A few minutes later, on North Fort Lauderdale Beach Boulevard, Luke asked a valet from a neighboring hotel where he could find some loose pussy that wouldn't require a credit card. The valet pointed inland and issued a warning.

"But you don't wanna go that way," he said. "Inland is the jungle, bro. Ask a cabbie where the kids hang out, you don't want to overpay. You got money, call an escort service. That's the safe bet. You want to chase, go anywhere along the beach, but be careful. Some guy staying here picked up a crack ho from the beach further south, got himself stabbed. Nothing too serious, but it could've been. The bitch was from Lauderdale Manors, an inland shithole of a neighborhood. Was in all the papers the next day."

The thought of picking up a crack ho by mistake was enough for

Palmieri to change his plans. He'd been with crack addicts before, but they had been dancers at a strip club in Queens he'd visited with Lou Testa, both white women who either danced at the club or slung drinks. Fucking the help was one of the perks wiseguys enjoyed, which put a big smile back on Palmieri's face. He was so close to getting straightened out he could taste it.

He decided to play it safe and headed back to the Ritz Carlton rather than out into the jungle. He looked through the telephone book for escort services and chose one with an exotic name. He ordered a girl for later the same night, but had to answer a series of questions before the woman on the other end of the line would take his credit card number.

Palmieri had dinner in his room before the escort, a Cuban woman in her mid-twenties with thick lips and an oversized boob-job, showed up. They had a few drinks and snorted some cocaine she'd brought. Then he had her blow him before he failed at reaching a second orgasm within the hour he'd paid for. Palmieri had to call the escort service to keep the Cuban for another hour. They had a few more drinks before he gave it another try, but all he'd gotten was close a few times before he gave up. He was suddenly feeling sleepy when he sent the woman off with a fifty dollar tip, something she wasn't happy about, the greedy twat.

Palmieri turned on the television and was barely awake when he thought he saw Lou Testa's picture on a local news channel. He tried to sit up but couldn't. He closed his eyes instead and slept for the next twenty-two hours.

■ ■ ■

Brooklyn/Staten Island, New York

Callahan took the call from Billings at a pizza parlor in Coney Island. He was thinking it was the best pizza he'd ever had when his cellphone rang. He took a bite from the crust he was holding before answering. Billings told him about Vito Calabrese and some of what he claimed he had to barter with.

"How's he giving up the old man if he was one of the two who tried to kill him?" Callahan said.

"He figures Adamo brokered the hit on Farese," Billings said.

"He figures or he knows?"

"What's the difference for now? We play along."

Callahan huffed. "You know about the retired cop, right?"

"Dalton," Billings said. "Had to be. He's looking for revenge. The cop
must've been on Cirelli's payroll. Wouldn't be the first dirty cop out
there. His wife was on the island, he probably dropped her off or something, then spotted Farese. And if Dalton has anything to do with Adamo,
and it appears that's the case, he might be looking to return the favor and
kill some of the Cirelli crew, the cop included."

"Or Cirelli himself," Callahan said. "Maybe we should approach him."

"There'll be a dozen buttons surrounding Cirelli after what happened
at the bar. Dalton's gotta be nuts to go after Cirelli now."

"Except they tried to kill him, too. Dalton, I mean. The other body at
Rye Harbor."

"You catch on quick, grasshopper."

Callahan ignored the wisecrack. "Why would the old man give up
Dalton now?"

"Maybe to save him," Billings said. "We won't know until you talk to
him. Give him some of the details. There's obviously a contract out on
Dalton by now."

"What else did Calabrese have to say?"

"Mostly bullshit, but he claims he has a tape in a safe deposit box. One
he made a few years back. Something to do with the Russian mob in
Brooklyn."

"So I'm going back to Staten Island?"

"I'll meet you there later. Get what you can from the old man. He
doesn't talk, fuck'em. Call me after you talk to him."

"Right," Callahan said.

He killed the call and immediately called Tommy Dalton's daughter.
There was no answer. He left a message for her to call him back. Ten minutes later he was crossing the Verrazano Narrows Bridge. Twenty minutes
after that he parked in the Staten Island hospital parking lot.

James Adamo was eating yogurt from a cup when Callahan entered his
room. "Ever eat this shit?" Adamo said. "It's not bad."

Callahan said, "One of the guys shot at you is looking to make a deal.
Vito Calabrese. Know him?"

"Which guy that shot at me is that?" Adamo said.

"The one that survived. It was a hit. For whatever you arranged in New
Hampshire probably."

"New Hampshire, that's in New England, right?"

"It comes back to Tommy Dalton. You know he has a daughter, right?" Adamo had been smirking. He lost the smirk.

"I met her," Callahan said. "She's a nice kid. Concerned about her father. She should be. Half the mob is probably out looking for him now, besides us and NYPD. You could help the kid out. Your friend too."

Adamo remained silent.

Callahan said, "Sooner or later, they'll have to finish what they started with you as well."

"That so?" Adamo said. "Who's they? My paisans? Eye-talians?"

"There's no audience here for the Walter Brennan routine, Mr. Adamo. Don't get me wrong, I could care less what you choose to do. Whatever gets me back home fastest is all I care about. Otherwise, you're just wasting my time."

"Walter Brennan, huh?" Adamo said. "Loved that guy in that Hemingway movie, the one from the book. *To Have and Have Not*, I think it was. I know he played a guy named Eddie. An old drunk or something."

"You done?" Callahan said.

"And the *Real McCoys*, too," Adamo said. "Brennan was great in that too."

"Right," Callahan said. He waved a hand and headed for the door. "Enjoy your yogurt."

As soon as he was outside the hospital, Callahan tried calling Alysha Dalton again, and again her voicemail picked up. This time he waited for the beep and said, "This is Special Agent Callahan again, Alysha. Please get back to me. It's important."

His phone rang before he was back to his car.

"Yeah?" he said.

"It's me," Billings said. "Stay where you are, I'm coming your way."

"I'm at the hospital."

"Wait there."

"What for?"

"Because I said so."

The call ended. Callahan cursed under his breath, reached into his pocket and pulled out the card Detective Kaprowski had given him back at the bar.

■ ■ ■

Brooklyn, New York

Tommy left his car in the Manhattan Beach parking lot and walked the length of Irwin Street to Shore Boulevard, crossed the Sheepshead Ford Bridge, and booked a room at a Best Western on Emmons Avenue. He showered and took a nap before watching the local news for updates on the two men he'd killed. Once both were confirmed associates of the Cirelli crime family, Tommy headed down to the business center to log onto Google.

He checked Google Maps to find out exactly where he was and to better familiarize himself with Brooklyn. Next he used the search engine to look up information on Frank Cirelli. There were several organized crime sites that provided a history of the Cirelli crime family, most of its members and associates, as well as a detailed bio of Gasper Cirelli and each of his four sons.

The eldest son, Angelo Sr., had died from cancer at age forty-one. The next eldest, Frank, had been running the crime family since his father's retirement a few years before he was released from federal prison the first time he went away. The father had gone back and was recently out again. The third son, Michael, had left the crime side of the family business and ran a popular restaurant in California. The youngest was Paul, age thirty-seven. Described as an over-ambitious gangster, Paul Cirelli was running crime family interests in South Florida.

Tommy found an address for Frank Cirelli on Staten Island. There was also an apartment in Manhattan under his youngest brother's name.

Tommy left the business center and took a walk along Emmons Avenue in search of someplace to eat. He recognized a restaurant name from Google, Randazzo's Clam Bar. He read the menu posted outside, saw that they delivered, and took one of the menu flyers back to the hotel. From his room he ordered a chicken parmagian with a sides of ziti and *zucchini*, and a six pack of Beck's beer.

Forty minutes later, Tommy watched the news while he ate dinner in his hotel room. There was nothing new about the two men he'd killed in Coney Island, but when a possible link was mentioned to the murder of a retired cop with the organized crime unit, Tommy headed back down to the business center to see what else he might learn on the Internet.

■ ■ ■

Brooklyn/Staten Island, New York

"Ouch, motherfucker!" Vito Calabrese yelled.

He was sitting forward, bent at the waist, his forehead touching the glove compartment in the passenger seat. His wrists had been cuffed to the adjuster bar underneath the front seat. His forehead scraped against the grain of the glove compartment each time the car hit a pothole, and Billings was aiming for them. He did so again now.

"Fuck!" Calabrese said. "This is bullshit, man. I'm taking pictures of my head soon as I'm out of this car."

They were on the Belt Parkway heading for Staten Island. Billings drove with his window open. The others were closed tight.

"At least put on the AC," Calabrese said. "I'm fucking dying here."

"Not yet," Billings said.

"Where the fuck we going? I want a lawyer."

"Going to meet your boss first," Billings said. "See what he thinks about us having you in custody. Who knows, maybe he'll flip too."

"Yeah, right, pal. Like you could take me to Cirelli."

Billings moved to the right lane and ran over a drain. The car bounced and Calabrese cursed under his breath.

Billings smiled. "What's that, Vito?"

"Cut it out!" Calabrese said.

Billings aimed for the next drain and ran over it too. "Don't feel so cocky now, do you?" he said. "The other night, all that tough guy talk. Where is it now?"

"I apologized for that already," Calabrese said.

Billings hit another drain.

"This shit you're pulling, it's gonna leave marks," Calabrese said.

Billings tapped the break hard enough to bounce Calabrese's head off the glove compartment.

"Jesus Christ, you're a sadist."

"I'll bet Lou Testa thinks so," Billings said.

"What?"

"Nothing. Point is, if Frank Cirelli is half as polite as you, I may take a walk for a cigarette while you two catch up."

"If you're waiting for me to shit my pants, you'll have to try harder. You're the law. You can't play that game with me."

"No, huh?" Billings spotted a chunk of asphalt missing up ahead and ran the right front tire over it. The car jolted from the pothole. Calabrese cursed again.

"Damn it, man. I can give you something with the Russians and Cirelli. I have it on tape."

"Yeah, you said. In a safe deposit box."

Calabrese tilted his head to the right in order to see Billings. "That's right," he said. "There's two tapes. One of Cirelli and some Russians and the other of Testa and Cirelli. Some other shit too, but it's small time stuff."

"And how'd you get those, assuming this isn't some desperate bullshit story."

"That'd be my business, but they're there. Two, three full tapes."

Billings nailed another drain. Calabrese bit his lower lip to suppress another cursing fit.

"They call these nickel rides in Philadelphia, what the law there gives pain in the ass perps like yourself," Billings said. "Put them in a van and hit every pothole they can find."

"It's fucked up is what it is," Calabrese said. "Police brutality."

Billings chuckled. "Let's just hope your wife didn't empty that safe deposit box out already. I mean, if you two are on the outs and all. She might've met somebody new by now, Vito. Taken all the cash, burned the tapes. Imagine?"

"She don't know about that box."

"Okay, so why don't we wait and see what Frank has to say first. I'm kind of interested to see what he'll do once he sees you."

"You're fucking crazy," Calabrese said. "You know that? You really are."

This time Billings jerked the steering wheel to the left, then right, and then back left again. Calabrese growled an inaudible curse.

■ ■ ■

Brooklyn, New York

There was nothing about the retired cop on the Internet yet, but Tommy found addresses for a few different men named Joe Collins in Baltimore. One in the Pigtown section looked promising. It wasn't a far trek from where the girls lived with their mother in Baltimore Highlands, a definite step up in neighborhoods. Collins couldn't have been happy when Sandi gave him the boot.

Tommy knew Collins worked at the Domino Sugar plant near the West Channel in Baltimore, but he wasn't sure if he'd get the opportunity to find him after he clipped Frank Cirelli. He could make the drive back to Baltimore and take care of Joe Collins first, but there was a chance he'd already been pegged as the shooter in New Hampshire. The cop who'd called Alysha was offering asylum Tommy would never accept. And it wasn't like the police in Baltimore didn't have his name. The question was whether or not they were sharing it with New York. The work he'd done with Gili more than ten years ago, and later the stabbing murder he'd done as a favor for Doc Adamo, had probably earned him a folder with FBI organized crime units in Maryland and New York.

He'd been questioned from time to time in Baltimore about the occasional Philadelphia wiseguy that had turned up dead, once near the ballpark at Camden Yards, and two other times closer to the docks on the waterfront, but Tommy had always been insulated from suspicion with concrete alibis. Still, the law knew his name, and it was just a matter of time before they found him.

If he wasn't already a primary suspect in the Farese murder, Tommy figured he had another day or two before he was. He'd have to deal with Joe Collins after Frank Cirelli. Baltimore was a few hours' drive. Staten Island was twenty minutes, maybe half an hour. Logistics solved the dilemma.

■ ■ ■

Staten Island, New York

Billings picked up Callahan outside the hospital parking lot. They moved Calabrese to the back seat and cuffed his wrists to the right rear front seat stanchion, then helped him bring his legs up onto and then across the back seat.

Billings followed the GPS directions to Hyland Boulevard, then drove south. It was quiet inside the car until Callahan asked Billings why Calabrese was with them.

"To see if we can shake Cirelli," Billings said. "He might not believe we have him otherwise."

"It's a little risky, no? You call for backup?"

"No need. Cirelli won't shoot the moron so long as we're there, although I'd almost pay to see it."

"You're a funny guy," Calabrese said.

"You try the girl again, Dalton's daughter?" Billings said.

"Voicemail," Callahan said.

"Who's Dalton?" Calabrese said.

"The guy we figure your boss hired to kill Dominick Farese."

"Which boss?"

"That's right," Billings said. "I almost forgot. You answered to Big Lou Testa, didn't you?"

"And he answered to Cirelli. That was the play, Testa didn't get killed."

"You know why that happened?" Callahan asked. He was looking at Billings.

"No clue," Calabrese said. "Unless he already had a deal nobody knew about."

Billings turned to Callahan and smiled. "One never knows, does one?"

The GPS directed a turn onto New Dorp Lane. A few GPS instructions later and they were climbing a sharp-curved road.

"Meisner Avenue," Billings read off a street sign. "This is it."

He pulled to the curb when he found the number he was looking for. A stocky man wearing sunglasses sat on the steps midway up to the porch of Frank Cirelli's home. Another man, tall and lean, stood on the porch. A steep stretch of woods was off to the left. Billings slid off the front seat. He glanced at Callahan and said, "Keep him company, but make sure he don't shit his pants, not inside the car."

Billings shut the door and crossed the road. Callahan watched him head toward a huge, gaudy-looking house. Billings was holding his identification out for the bodyguard on the stairs. The bodyguard held up a hand, but Billings brushed it aside and continued up the stairway to the front porch. The tall man was holding a shotgun. Billings held up his identification again. The tall man looked it over, then rang the bell.

"He's fuckin' nuts, your boss," Calabrese said to Callahan.

Callahan watched as the front door to the house opened. A short boxy woman stood in the doorway. She gave a hard look at the tall man. Billings held up his identification yet again. The woman was about to shut the door when a tall, curly haired man Callahan assumed was Frank Cirelli stopped her. He and Billings had a brief conversation before the door opened wider and Billings stepped inside the house.

Callahan quickly dialed Kaprowski's number on his cellphone. The detective answered and Callahan gave their location. The detective said he was fifteen, maybe twenty minutes away.

"Who was that?" Calabrese asked.

"Reinforcements," Callahan said.

"Your crazy boss really trying to deal with Cirelli like this, at his home?"

Callahan said, "What did you say to him on the phone the other night?"

"To who, happy up there?"

"Who'd you tell him you could deal away?"

Calabrese shrugged. "I don't know. Testa, for one, but I got a tape with something else."

Callahan said, "What did you tell him about Testa?"

"Nothing specific. I wasn't saying shit until I had a deal. Why?"

Callahan looked back up at the house. The bodyguards were having a conversation, but Billings was gone and the door was closed again. Then the stocky bodyguard returned to his position midway down the stairs.

"The fuck is going on?" Calabrese said. "He going in for coffee?"

■ ■ ■

The wife had answered the door, but it was Frank Cirelli who spoke to the federal agent.

"Where's Brennan?" he said.

"He's New York," Billings said. "I'm from up north. New England."

"And?"

"I was wondering if we could talk a few minutes. Exchange ideas maybe."

"About what?"

"Listen to what I have to say and then we'll see."

Cirelli took a deep breath. He let it out slow, then stepped further back behind the door as he opened it. Billings stepped inside the house and

Cirelli closed the door behind him.

"Tell you the truth, I expected a few more bodyguards," Billings said.

Cirelli ignored the comment and pointed to the living area. Billings crossed the hall and took a seat on a large beige leather couch. He noticed a shotgun leaning against an end table and motioned at it with his head.

"Scare off the birds?" he said.

"Something like that," Cirelli said. He sat in a dark brown recliner to the left of the couch.

"So, how're things?" Billings said.

Cirelli smiled.

"It's lame, I know," Billings said, "but I'm wondering you want to walk it in now. Can't be much of a future with what's happened. You're a boss, so you'd get the best of the perks."

"Isn't this Brennan's job, trying to flip me?"

"Yeah, but I'm here now. Brennan's probably got his hands full. You left quite the mess behind Farese. A retired cop, the two in New Hampshire, Testa here, and the two in the bar. Not to mention the piece of shit sitting outside in the car."

"Which piece of shit is that?"

"Calabrese. You had to know he'd make his play once you missed him at Grand Central. He told us about it, how Testa was there following some dancer Calabrese'd been poking."

Cirelli gave it a moment.

Billings said, "Look, you're vulnerable now. Whatever Calabrese has to offer is just the start. Chances are the other bosses won't risk your defection anyway. We both know you have two ways out of this cluster fuck and one of them is with you catching a couple behind the head. The other is the way everybody else chooses these days. You flip, at least you live. And you wouldn't be the first boss to make a deal."

"That the real reason you came here tonight, to see if I'd flip?"

"Honestly?"

Cirelli smiled as he shrugged this time.

"This was grandstanding coming here," Billings said. "Maybe it convinces the moron in the car to start talking now before he talks to a lawyer. He's insisting on one, the asshole. You should've heard his smart mouth the night they patched his call through to me. Offered Testa on a silver platter, said he has more. A couple of tapes in a safe deposit box. We're supposed to get them tomorrow, but he'll want a lawyer in on that for sure.

Apparently the tough guy has been reading up on how to make a deal. Told me he wants to live someplace warm. I hung up on him. Now he's willing to wear a sweater, gloves and earmuffs, doesn't care where we send him. He's more afraid of dying, I guess."

"You the guy called the bar?" Cirelli said. "About Testa, I mean."

Billings' brow furrowed. "Not sure what you're talking about."

"I'll take that as a yes."

"Anyway, unless he spewed to the agent babysitting him out there, or unless you come out with that shotgun in your hand, Calabrese won't talk until he gets his lawyer. Then, if he has anything on you, he'll be more than happy to fork it over."

Cirelli looked at his watch.

Billings said, "Hey, you can't blame me for trying."

■ ■ ■

Billings stepped out onto the porch of Frank Cirelli's house in time to see three police cruisers pulling up to the curb. Another car was parked in front of the one he'd driven to Staten Island. Special Agent Callahan was talking to the NYPD detective they'd met on the beach. Billings couldn't remember his name. Both bodyguards were at the bottom of the stairs, the tall one clutching the shotgun.

"I'd put that down before you get clipped," Billings told him.

Four of NYPD's finest already had their guns drawn. The tall man set the shotgun on the floor.

Billings yelled at Callahan and the detective across Meisner Avenue. "The fuck is this about?"

The detective turned and smiled. "Special Agent," he said. "How you doing tonight?"

"What the fuck is this?" Billings said.

"I'm Kaprowski," the detective said. "Ovie, remember? We're taking Vito Calabrese into custody."

"Like hell you are."

"He's wanted for an attempted murder he's admitting to and you'll probably get him back anyway, but not until we book him. Sorry."

"The fuck you think you're talking to, sonny?"

"Go fuck yourself," Kaprowski said. Another car pulled up to the curb. "Here they are," he said. "They're mine, organized crime. They'll be tak-

ing Calabrese with them. You can follow along or arrange to meet up tomorrow. Your choice."

"I'll have your ass on this," Billings said.

"I'm sure you'll try," Kaprowski said.

Billings' jaw clenched as Calabrese was walked to the back of the car that
had just pulled up. He stood stone-faced as one of the squad cars pulled
away followed by the unmarked car. The other two squad cars remained
at the curb.

Billings glared at the driver behind the wheel of one of the squad cars before turning to Callahan. "They follow us?"

Callahan shrugged.

"Fuck this," Billings said. "Let's go."

Both men returned to their car. Billings drove.

Ft. Lauderdale, Florida

It wasn't until after his shower when Luke Palmieri realized he'd been
drugged. He'd woken up with a bad headache and went straight to the
bathroom to relieve himself and take a shower, but when he stepped
back out of the bathroom he saw the room was a mess. All the drawers had
been emptied and the portable safe was opened.

Palmieri paced back and forth pulling at his hair and cursing under his
breath. How could he have been so stupid? How could he have left the safe
unlocked?

He sat on the edge of the bed and tried his best to remember what had
happened the night before, whether he'd stashed his money in the safe or
not. Everything was a blur. Whatever that bitch had slipped him in his
drink, he couldn't remember shit.

His wallet was empty, including all the credit cards, real and stolen.

He could call his mother and get her to send him money to get home,
but he was supposed to stay there and meet with Paul Cirelli at some point.
How they hell could he explain getting rolled by a hooker to made guys?

"Fuck," he said. "Fuck, fuck, fuck, fuck, fuck."

He picked up the phone and dialed his mother collect. He started to tell
her what happened when she apologized about his friend.

"What friend, Ma? The hell are you talkin' about?"

"Mr. Testa," she said. "It's all over the news. He was killed the other day.

I assumed you knew."

Luke Palmieri felt his stomach emptying before he could excuse himself.

■ ■ ■

Manhattan, New York

"It's turned into a big waste of time," Billings told his wife over the phone, "but now that some New York detective fucked with me, I'd like to make some trouble for him."

"What kind of trouble?"

"The heavy kind, political. He pulled some jurisdictional crap on me last night. I intend to return the favor."

"Then come home and do it from here," his wife said. "Put your papers in now. You don't need it anymore."

It was the truth, he didn't need it anymore, except this time he'd been effective in getting rid of at least one asshole. Lou Testa's death was a small victory Billings could still savor. Shooting down Calabrese's deal had almost made the trip to New York worthwhile. At least until last night. The NYPD detective, Kaprowski, had pushed the wrong buttons.

"May is bringing the kids this weekend," his wife said. "They're down from Montreal. I'd think you'd want to spend some time with your grandchildren, Peter. It's been six months."

She was right about the grandchildren too, but there was still a chance he could leave a mark on his way into retirement. Frank Cirelli would be hounded by the New York Special Agent in Charge, Joseph Brennan. Billings was thinking he might be able to play the good cop to Brennan's bad, if he wasn't told to head back home. There was a chance he'd get that call sometime later in the day.

"Your daughter will be very disappointed if you're not here," his wife said, bringing him back to their conversation. "I hope you know that."

"I do," Billings said. "I know. I'll do my best, I promise. There's a mob war of some kind going on here, what it looks like. Watch the news today, I'm sure they'll cover it."

His wife huffed on her end of the line.

"What do you want from me, Grace?" Billings said. "It's my job."

"Right," she said. "Let me know what you're going to do when you know. I have to tell them something."

Immediately after the call ended, another agent from the New York office filled him in on the Quinlan King murder in Brooklyn. Billings was waiting to hear about Calabrese and the NYPD, but nothing was mentioned.

He called Special Agent Callahan's room to wake him up. Half an hour later they met in the lobby. Callahan was toting his travel bag.

"What's this?" Billings said.

"I'm out," Callahan said. "Going home."

"Excuse me?"

"I'm leaving the Bureau, Pete. I'm done with this. I don't like it and I miss my wife. I already missed our anniversary. I don't intend to miss sleeping with her tonight."

"Just like that? You do know there's protocol, I hope."

"I'll do whatever they ask," Callahan said. "Exit interview, whatever. I'm going back to police work I can live with. This bullshit I can't live with. Life is too short."

"The retired cop in Brooklyn is the guy gave up Farese," Billings said.

Callahan had already learned about the retired cop's tie to New Hampshire from Kaprowski, but he wasn't about to engage Billings in that conversation. "Great," he said. "Now you can go home too."

"His wife was on the island, has been all week. They're checking tapes at the dock where the boat leaves for the island in Portsmouth, but the cop had pictures of Farese on his and his wife's cell phone. He took her there. It's him."

"I heard you the first time, Pete."

"The cop's house was trashed," Billings said.

"I know. Kaprowski told me, remember? I was with him at the bar in Coney Island."

"Somebody looking for cash is my guess, but he probably put most of that someplace safer than his house. He's the guy gave up Farese. Cirelli is still looking to sever all ties."

"Like Testa, or was that us?"

"Excuse me?"

Callahan shook his head. "Forget it. I've got a plane to catch."

Billings put his hand up. "Wait," he said. "The hell is that supposed to mean, like us?"

"Nothing. I've got a plane to catch."

"I hope you didn't—"

"I didn't. Now, excuse me."

Billings didn't move. Callahan stepped around him and headed for the revolving doors.

■ ■ ■

Brooklyn, New York

Tommy ate breakfast in his room before calling the front desk to arrange for a car rental. He watched the local news but learned nothing new about the retired cop who'd been killed in his own home. He turned off the television and read a *USA Today*. He read another article about Mo'Ne Davis, the 13-year-old girl who'd pitched a shutout in the Little League World Series. She'd already been featured on the cover of *Sports Illustrated*. Tommy was thinking he'd like to read more about the kid.

Next he read about the Mets and the Yankees, and how major league baseball was finding a big decline in attendance. One columnist insisted it was the result of the A-Rod fiasco the year before; that Major League Baseball's persecution of the Yankee slugger had turned people off. The ultimate bullshit, Tommy thought. The same league that had turned a blind eye to steroids for years, allowing a home run race that brought all kinds of extra attention and attendance to the game, was suddenly acting as if it gave a crap about its image beyond dollars and cents.

"Try lowering the price of tickets," Tommy said.

He turned the page and searched for his home team box score. The Cubs had beaten the Orioles again. Tommy shook his head. He hated the interleague play, but losing to the Cubs somehow made it even worse.

He remembered the story his street rabbi Gili had once told him about the Orioles losing to the Mets in the '69 World Series, and how some kid who'd been having an affair with the wrong woman was thrown from the roof of Memorial Stadium. It was a few months after hearing that story when Tommy started paying attention to the Orioles. He wasn't a big sports fan by any stretch, but he enjoyed keeping track of his home team.

Gili had told him a few stories that day, the same day Gili killed a wiseguy from New York as a favor to a Philadelphia Mob boss. It was Tommy's first big payday working for mobsters. The New York wiseguy had been hired to kill the cheating wife of a big shot's son and her lover.

Killing the wiseguy was part of eliminating loose ends, and had been approved by the New York Mob. Tommy had been backup, sitting in the back seat in case something went wrong. Gili did the shooting, but legally it was Tommy's introduction to murder.

Several years later, when the son of the boss who had ordered the hit flipped and tried to implicate him and Gili for murder, Tommy lucked out when the snitch hung himself in a protective custody cell.

Tommy wondered what the hell had been going through the poor bastard's mind before he killed himself. Was he too weak to deal with the short amount of jail time he'd have to do? Was he ashamed of being a snitch? Was it his wife's infidelity that haunted him? Was it her death at the hands of his father's orders?

Or was he just tired of living.

Tommy remembered his last conversation with Doc and how his friend had wondered if Tommy was tired of living.

■ ■ ■

Miami, Florida

"The fuck is going on?" Paul Cirelli asked his brother. "I'm waitin' three days already."

Paul was responding to an emergency call from his brother earlier in the day. Each brother, one in New Jersey, the other in Miami, had to call from a secure phone line. The telephone tag had started early in the morning; Frank leaving messages for Paul to expect his call around noon. Paul had left return messages requesting the call later in the afternoon. The messages went back and forth between third parties until Paul agreed to a three o'clock call.

"What's going on is I got a fucking mess on my hands," Frank told his brother. "Half the feds in this city and a couple they imported from New England. Last night the local O.C. picked up Calabrese. He couldn't wait to make a deal. The locals took him from the feds, but you know he'll be getting a retirement package soon enough. He got his button with you, kid. It's not good."

"I remember," Paul said.

"You hear what happened in Coney Island?"

"I got a call, yeah. You got an idea yet?"

"Yeah, but there's nothing I can do until he comes out."

"Redfellas?"

"No, no way. This is something else. The guy I figure for the bar. He's playing with fire, though. All the attention around here now."

"You know the guy, take him out."

"Easier said than done."

"Anything I can do from here?"

"Actually, there is. That other guy I told you about, the kid, he's there now. Should be. Ft. Lauderdale, not far from you."

"The kid I'm supposed to meet, yeah."

"I'm wondering maybe he's nervous, that thing with Testa the other day back here. Maybe he's spooked. He did what I asked, but you never know."

"You want this taken care of or what?"

"Can you feel him out first, see what's what with this kid?"

"This my brother I'm speaking to?"

"Excuse me?"

"Somethin' the old man used to say. You gotta' think about it, there's nothin' to think about."

Frank went silent.

"You there?" Paul said.

"Yeah."

"Whatta'ya wanna do?"

"Trade places."

Paul chuckled. "Maybe six weeks ago."

"You're supposed to be the ambitious one."

"I learned to read."

"Meaning?"

"Not interested. Everybody makes deals now. That guy you're worried about, maybe he did too. Maybe he's thinking about it. He here on a promise?"

"Yeah, but that can't happen now. He doesn't know it, but after this mess, the books'll stay closed for a while. A long while."

"So long as he doesn't know it."

Frank huffed on his end of the line. "Look, all I'm saying, he disappears, no harm, no foul."

Paul chuckled again. "Unless you think this guy down here is one of the good ones. Personally, I don't think there's any such animal anymore. Feds don't make it a difficult choice. The rest of your life in the joint or cut a deal."

"Yeah, and we can expect it'll be Calabrese next."

"Thanks for reminding me," Paul said.

"Sorry."

"There's nothing to consider, this other guy, the kid down here."

"I guess not. You're right."

"Then consider it done."

"Alright, good. Thanks."

Paul Cirelli killed the call and turned to the special agent standing alongside him. "Okay? Happy now?"

"Very," the special agent said. "Good job. Before you know it, you'll be back in New York running things, compliments of Uncle Sam."

"Doesn't make me proud," Cirelli said. "Just so you know."

■ ■ ■

Brooklyn, New York

Tommy wiped sweat from his brow as he walked along the water on Emmons Avenue. It was a muggy night. The forecast called for rain, a temporary break in the heat wave. He watched a group of young girls across the Avenue. They stood in a circle giggling. He thought of his daughters, all three of them this time, and decided to call Alysha again. The phone rang five times before her voice mail answered. He shut his phone off and continued walking.

The sea smell became a fishy odor when he approached the charter boats advertising daily fishing trips for bluefish, porgy, fluke, sea bass and blackfish. There were day and night trips, as well as party charters. Tommy had gone fishing once in his life and swore he'd never go again.

That had been on a boat out of Maryland's Chesapeake Bay when he was fifteen years old. The smell of the bait being churned into chum made him sick before the boat left the harbor. He hadn't eaten breakfast before they left, leaving him with dry heaves until he gave up and tried to sleep off the trip on a bench on the top deck of the boat. Six hours later, once the boat returned to dock and it was time to get off, Tommy could still feel the waves. He felt it back at home in the shower, and again when he tried to eat dinner the same night.

He still didn't understand the point of paying to get sick or to stand on a rocking boat holding onto a fishing rod. His father, an avid fisherman all his life, had wanted to share his love of the sport with his son, but the trip had been a disaster Tommy was never allowed to live down. The ribbing started at dinner that night and had lasted until his father died.

It was his past he was thinking about as he continued walking along Emmons Avenue, how he'd gone from a kid getting sick on a fishing trip to a hired killer. After a while he stopped and leaned on the railing overlooking the bay. He tried to clear his thoughts. There was no point in reliving the past. He'd gone from good to bad, and then bad to worse. Talking to Alysha again now would only require him to lie some more. He'd said his piece. He'd made his bed and now he'd pay for it.

Besides, he couldn't explain his life to her any more than he could justify it to himself. He'd made choices as a young man he couldn't take back, but it was his lack of being around for his daughters that upset him most.

Nor could he afford to regret anything. It was time to take Frank Cirelli out and then he would try to get back to Baltimore to settle one last score. Then, if it was possible afterward, he might get out of the country. Maybe.

■ ■ ■

Ft. Lauderdale, Florida

"Don't I get a lawyer?" Luke Palmieri said.

He'd been about to head down to the front desk to see if his mother had wired him money for his return flight to New York when there was a knock on the door. He'd spent most of the day anticipating the worst because of what had happened to Lou Testa. He couldn't wait to get home, except then he intended to take off again, probably in the opposite direction. He wasn't crazy about going to Canada, but New York would remain too dangerous to stick around.

Palmieri had become a nervous wreck since he woke up and discovered he'd been drugged and robbed, and possibly in the middle of a mob war. He didn't understand how or why Lou Testa was killed and he was afraid to call the restaurant in Little Italy to ask about it. So when he answered the knock at the door, Palmieri nearly fainted when he saw three men holding up their FBI identifications. Two of the agents had come in the room to help him to the bed. The other agent remained in the hall.

Now he was sitting on the edge of the bed in a state of confused shock. The agent doing the talking, a guy named Crawford, showed Palmieri an electronic recorder and told him to take a seat. Then he played a recording of two men he claimed were the Cirelli brothers, Frank and Paul.

"That other guy I told you about, the kid, he's there now. Should be. Ft. Lauderdale, not far from you. He was told you'd call him. Now I'm wondering maybe he's nervous, that thing with the big guy back here. Maybe he's spooked. He did what I asked, but you never know."

"You want this taken care of or what?"

"Can you feel him out first, see what's what with this kid?"

"This my brother I'm speaking to?"

"Excuse me?"

"Somethin' the old man used to say. You gotta' think about it, there's nothin' to think about."

Crawford stopped the tape. "You know who they're talking about yet?"

Palmieri swallowed hard. "How do I know that tape isn't edited?"

Crawford pressed PLAY.

"Everybody makes deals now. That guy you're worried about, maybe he did too. Maybe he's thinking about it. He here on a promise?"

"Yeah, but that can't happen now. He doesn't know it, but after this mess, the books'll stay closed for a while. A long while."

"So long as he doesn't know it."

"Look, all I'm saying, he disappears, no harm, no foul."

Crawford stopped the recorder again.

"You heard the tape and still think you need one, a lawyer?" Special Agent Crawford said. "Last night Vito Calabrese was booked by the NYPD on an attempted murder charge. He'd already talked to us about a deal. He has anything, he'll get one. The Cirellis are nervous, kid. You try and stand up, there may not be anybody around to give you a button when you get out. Frank Cirelli is cleaning his mess and you're obviously on the list."

"I never met Frank Cirelli," Palmieri said.

"You never needed to," Crawford said. "He wants you taken out, we'll assume it's important to him you go. You can explain it to us or not, but understand that if Cirelli himself cuts a deal, and he's bound to sooner or later, they all do, you're the one who'll be on the outside looking in."

"Jesus fuckin' Christ, I don't know what to do," Palmieri said. He was holding his head with both hands.

"Look, kid, you don't need a lawyer yet," Crawford said. "We're not arresting you. We have a tape discussing your demise."

Palmieri swallowed hard.

"Yeah," Crawford said, "it's a scary conversation. They're talking about whacking you down here. Killing you because they're in a panic up north. You just heard some of it. You can talk to us, a federal prosecutor, or a lawyer. That's your choice, except the lawyer you'll have to call on your own unless you're going to deal with us. My job was to warn you about a death threat. You weren't associated with the Cirelli people, nobody in the bureau would've known who you are."

"And what if the guy who told me to do something was already dead?" Palmieri said. "Then where am I?"

"First off, it depends on what you did," Crawford said. "Second, maybe they keep you on the street, book you on some bogus bullshit, hide you a while, then release you so you have a cover. It's been done before."

Palmieri was shaking his head.

"Or what you did lands you a jail term," Crawford said. "If so, and you cooperate, you'll likely be in protective custody, outside general population."

"Likely?"

"Probably."

"Fuck man, you're not giving me much here."

Crawford sat back in the chair. "You need some time to think about it, we'll remain posted outside your door, but at some point, kid, we're gonna have to leave."

The special agent stood up, then pointed at the recorder again. "You want, you can listen to that a few more times. I'll come back for it, but we have plenty copies, in case you try and burn it."

He started for the door.

Palmieri stopped him. "No, wait," he said. "What do I have to do?"

■ ■ ■

Staten Island, New York

Doc knew there was something wrong earlier in the evening. His neuralgia had woken him from a deep sleep before dinner and stayed with him
on and off throughout the night. He was to be discharged the next morning. He felt lightheaded and skipped dinner, and then the neuralgia returned, except this time it was severe. The streaking pain precluded him
from moving. The last thing he wanted was to remain in the hospital, but
the pain was intense. There was a shift change of nurses shortly after midnight when he collapsed in his bed.

He remained unconscious for several minutes before he was able to open
his eyes again. When he did, he saw that he was surrounded by a team of
physicians and nurses.

"Can you hear me?" one of the doctors said.

Doc wasn't able to speak yet. He did his best to nod.

"Are you still in pain?"

Doc nodded again.

"We're going to bring you upstairs for some tests. We think you may've
had a stroke, Mr. Adamo."

Before he could respond another sharp pain caused him to cringe.

Then he heard the words Code Blue before he was overcome by a
numbing sensation. He felt hands probing his neck, then something cold
on his chest. He felt his body jerk, but could no longer hear. His eyes remained opened as his head turned to the right. The last thing he saw was
his wife standing in the doorway looking stunned.

Brooklyn/Staten Island, New York

Tommy set out for Staten Island at 3:30 in the morning. Armed with bug
spray, rubber gloves, a navy blue Yankees cap, a few Snickers bars, a
small cooler filled with ice, six bottles of water, and the Google map he'd
printed in the business center of the hotel, he following the rental's GPS
instructions and crossed the Verrazano Narrows Bridge into Staten Island.
Tommy followed the flow of the zigzagging road on the Staten Island Expressway. Miles of construction on both sides of the road had rerouted the
driving lanes with solid white lines rather than dashed ones. Tommy

picked the middle lane and kept within the speed limit until he spotted the
exit for 440 near the end of the expressway. To the left was the Goethals
Bridge to New Jersey. Tommy stayed in the middle lane and veered right.
There was no traffic on 440, but Tommy kept within the 50 miles per
hour speed limit. The drive on 440 was a short one. He stayed in the left
lane to avoid the turnoff for the Outerbridge Crossing. He followed the
signs onto the Korean War Veterans Memorial Parkway. Twelve minutes
later, he was turning right onto Arthur Kill Road. He followed the GPS
directions until he spotted a Dunkin Donuts in a strip mall. Tommy
pulled into the parking lot.

He was back in the car after picking up half a dozen donuts and two coffees. He'd circled two areas on the Google map to the right of Meisner Avenue on Lighthouse Hill, an area on the map that appeared to be mostly
trees. He needed to find a spot close enough to Frank Cirelli's home so he
could kill him from cover. Tommy ate two donuts and finished one of the
two coffees before he was back on the road.

He used the GPS to guide him to Lighthouse Avenue. The next mile or
so was mostly uphill, the road twisting and turning, mostly sharp curves
lined with expensive homes. Tommy drove at the 25 miles per hour
speed limit, slowing down for the speed bumps and the treacherous
curves, the last of which left him on Meisner Avenue. He saw three
NYPD squad cars parked along the curb in front of Frank Cirelli's address
and wondered what the fuck that was about. He couldn't slow down to
check it out more carefully, but he did spot two men who didn't look like
cops standing at the foot of the stairs. He continued along the road until
he was heading down a steep hill with one more sharp turn. There was no
room to park along the side of the road. A traffic light was straight ahead
at the end of the hill, but a sign for a Nursing Home caught his eye. He
turned right into the driveway and pulled to the side of the road to check
his bearings.

Frank Cirelli lived on the next to last stretch of Meisner Avenue. Tommy
could access the woods in front of the house from the nursing home, either through the parking lot or from the driveway. He considered it a
stroke of luck, but he'd need a better escape route than passing in front of
Cirelli's home after shooting him. There were three different directions he
could head after making a right out of the nursing home driveway. There
were also several different parking lots adjacent to the facility. All of them
lead to more wooded areas.

Tommy listened to the radio while parked in the driveway. A weather forecast called for more humidity and possible thunderstorms during the day. There was more about the expected protests in the city and some political bullshit about Syria and terrorism.

A string of commercials for Internet backup systems followed. Tommy switched stations. He was about to start the engine and decide on one of the nursing home parking lots when a news station reported the sudden death of the sixty-seven year old Vietnam veteran who was shot and wounded earlier in the week outside the Heartland Village shopping center. James Adamo had died from a brain aneurism.

Tommy turned the radio off.

"Fuck," he said.

He checked his watch and saw it was almost five o'clock in the morning. He needed to make his trek through the woods and station himself in front of Frank Cirelli's house before dawn. Then he'd kill however much time it took before the wiseguy stepped outside his house. He hoped it would be early enough so that he could backtrack out of the woods to his car under the cover of darkness, but he wasn't counting on it.

And if Cirelli showed himself before dawn, Tommy was thinking he'd use the laser sighting on his rifle to give the wiseguy a moment of terror just before he killed him.

■ ■ ■

Ovie Kaprowski presented his shield as he walked into the social club across from Miller Field on New Dorp Lane. Gasper Cirelli, a cigar jammed in his mouth, was playing cards at one of three tables. The game was Acey Deucey. Kaprowski was guessing there was at least two thousand dollars in the middle of the table.

"We need to talk," he said to Gasper Cirelli.

"Now?" the old man said without looking up from his cards.

"Now," Kaprowski said.

"Can you wait out this hand?"

"No. I have a family to get home to. Let's go."

"And if I don't?"

"Then I'll say what I have to say in front of your friends and embarrass you."

Gasper huffed, cursed under his breath, and set his cards face down on the table. "Sorry fellas," he told the other players. "I'll be right back."

They walked outside the social club, then crossed the street. The old man leaned against the window of a parked car. Kaprowski stood a few feet away facing him.

Gasper removed the cigar from his mouth and said, "What's it about?"

"Three things," Kaprowski said. "In case you didn't hear yet, we have Vito Calabrese."

The old man showed no reaction, except to turn his head away from Kaprowski.

"I'll assume you do know," Kaprowski said. "Number two, there's a contract on your son."

Gasper looked up. "Where'd you hear that?"

"Somebody with the Vignieri crew. I know Frank met with them the other day, but things have changed since word is out about Calabrese making a deal. Between the killings, the botched attempts and now Calabrese, it makes sense they're assuming the worst."

"And what's that?"

Kaprowski held up three fingers. "Third, the old man died a few hours ago. Jimmy Adamo."

"Jimmy who?" Gasper said.

"Look, I'm not looking to play games here. Frank cuts a deal or not, I could care less, but if they hit Frank, chances are they'll look to take you out too."

"The Vignieri crew has its own problems," Gasper said. "The others? Let them try."

"This isn't time for talking tough, old man. You can do your own damage, you want. Protect whatever's left of this shit operation you built. Protect what's important, your family."

"You smoking that crack shit or something? I got nothing to say to you or anybody else with a badge."

"Or you can watch your kid go down one way or the other. Maybe you're next. You and I both know the feds are gonna come around tomorrow offering the same deal. Tomorrow might be too late. You do the right thing now, I've got two cars out in front of Frank's house. I'll keep them there until the marshals arrive."

The old man looked at Kaprowski as if he were insane. "We done?"

Kaprowski raised both hands.

Gasper Cirelli shook his head, chuckled, and then made his way back across the street into the social club. Kaprowski called headquarters and ordered the protection removed from Frank Cirelli's house.

■ ■ ■

The two police cruisers were still parked across the street from Cirelli's house, and the two guys that looked like bodyguards were there too; one sitting on the steps and the other leaning against the porch railing. Tommy wondered if Cirelli had cut a deal, except why would the bodyguards still be there? The police might be there to protect the rest of Cirelli's family, but if Frank Cirelli was already in a federal safe house somewhere, Tommy was out of luck. There was no way to know without waiting to see what was what.

There was more than enough brush to build the blind. Tommy found a good position near a tree stump from where he could see the Cirelli home clearly. His line of sight through the scope covered the front door and the driveway. He used broken branches with and without leaves to camouflage the blind.

When he finished, Tommy sat on another tree stump a few feet from the blind. He watched intermittent traffic passing on the avenue up above. He checked his watch and saw it was 5:45 a.m. The sun would be up in another hour or so.

He smashed a mosquito against his neck. A trace of blood stained his left palm. He watched the road again and wondered about his friend Doc. He hoped his death was the painless one Doc had once wished for; that he'd die in his sleep, a death Tommy never imagined for himself. He was sure that when it was his time, it would be violent. He'd signed up for it a long time ago. He also felt he deserved whatever violence was coming his way. The trick was not losing one's composure anticipating the end.

If there was an afterlife, if it was what he'd been taught as a young Catholic kid growing up in Baltimore, Tommy had no doubt he'd wind up in hell.

And if there wasn't an afterlife, what he'd believed for most of his life, then his only regrets would remain with the father he hadn't been to his girls.

Tommy heard a scuffling somewhere behind him and was surprised to see an adult deer darting through the woods. He was confused. Staten Island was small on the Google map, but dense with population, almost half a million people. Even in the short time he was there, he could tell the place would swarm with traffic come rush hour. He wondered how deer survived in such a populated area. How did they manage to avoid getting hit by all the vehicular traffic?

Back in Catholic school, he'd been taught that when the young died, especially children, no matter whether they were good or not, they were given a pass and granted instant access to heaven. Tommy preferred to believe that bad luck always ran its course, so when the young died, children or deer, they'd merely been caught in the wrong place at the wrong time.

He was starting to feel sleepy when he heard car engines starting. He looked up and saw the police cruisers come to life a few seconds apart. Their headlights flashed on and both made K-turns at the same time before driving off.

Tommy wondered what was going on until he spotted headlights returning from the same direction the police cruisers had just driven off to on Meisner Road. He moved back to the blind when the car slowed in front of Cirelli's house. A horn beeped and the car turned into the Cirelli driveway. The bodyguard was up off his ass now. Tommy grabbed the rifle, dropped to a knee, and looked through the scope.

■ ■ ■

A woman opened the front door when she heard the horn. She was wearing a bathrobe. She stood in the doorway looking down at the car.

An elderly man stepped out of the car, his back to the street. He carried two plastic bags containing groceries, it looked like, or maybe bagels and milk.

The woman stepped out onto the porch and called to the man. He looked up. Words were exchanged. The man held up the plastic bags and she waved at him to come up. The bodyguard on the stoop took the plastic bags from the old man, then followed him up the stairs. Frank Cirelli suddenly appeared in the doorway. A second later, a single shot took off the top of his head. The woman screamed when Cirelli's body hit the porch floor. The old man and bodyguard dropped to their knees. A second shot hit the bodyguard on the stairs in the middle of his back. A third shot struck the bodyguard standing on the porch in the neck before he could aim the shotgun he was holding. The old man had crawled onto the porch, but the woman seemed to push off his back, knocking him to the floor again before running inside the house. She slammed the door shut behind her.

■   ■   ■

Tommy understood that he was never dealing with men of honor early on in his criminal career. What he didn't learn from his street rabbi, Gili Thomasso, he learned firsthand on the street and in prison. The criminal badge of honor was a crock of shit. Most of the mob guys he'd dealt with were nothing more than opportunistic sociopaths, bullies and thugs. The ones who managed to hold their water and do their time without making deals were fewer and further between. The old school mobsters had died off a long time ago. The new kids on the block were way too soft and way too weak to handle prison. Or maybe they were too smart. Who wouldn't make a trade that kept you outside?

Tommy had seen them fold in the BCDC during his incarceration. The guys you could almost guarantee would flip were the ones who dragged a finger across their throat when discussing snitches. "Should cut their throats, the rat cocksuckers," he once heard a wannabe in Philadelphia say, a guy who was quick to cut a deal the first time he was facing serious time.

It was one reason he followed Gili's advice to never attach himself to one of the crime families operating out of Philadelphia. There was no way to trust them.

Over the years, he'd read about mob fathers given up by their sons and vice versa. It was the same thing all over—mobsters, drug dealers, street gangs and dirty cops. It was all bullshit.

Gili used to joke about Tommy being blessed for having Irish parents. Gili used to tell him he was lucky he couldn't get made. "Cuts down on the guys'll give you up. You're a gun for hire, you're careful, push ever comes to shove you stand a chance that way. Most times, you hire a good enough lawyer, you're home free."

It was what he'd been thinking about before killing Frank Cirelli, maybe to justify another murder. At least he was hearing Gili's voice in his head as he squeezed off the shot that took the top of Frank Cirelli's head off. He was thinking about escaping a moment later when he rapidly refocused his gun sight on the bodyguards one at a time and took care of them. Then he was running through the woods towards the nursing home, thinking he just might make it back to Baltimore after all.

■ ■ ■

Manhattan, New York

Billings heard about Frank Cirelli's murder from the New York office of
the FBI. He was told he was no longer needed and that he could return
home. When he asked about Special Agent Callahan's status, he was
told to call his home bureau in Boston.

"Fuck you too," he said after the call.

He wasn't sure what Callahan might've surmised from Lou Testa's murder, but it couldn't be more than conjecture. Billings had disguised his
voice, whether there was a bug in the Cirelli bar or not. He'd walked to
First Avenue to make the call, three full blocks north of the United Nations. There was no way anybody could link him to that phone call.

Besides, the kid wasn't happy with the job. Maybe he wanted out and
their relationship had been the last straw. Maybe the kid preferred writing tickets back in Concord, New Hampshire.

So fuck him.

Billings phoned his wife and told her he'd be home as soon as he could
book a flight and get to the airport. He'd land in Boston and take a cab to
their home in Cambridge. He asked if their daughter was still there, then
realized it was the wrong question. He'd be in the dog house for at least
the next week once he was home. It almost made him grateful he'd have
to answer four thousand questions about the investigation. What had happened in New Hampshire and later in New York would keep him busy
through the week, and he'd still have to sweat out whatever Callahan might
say. They'd ask him about that too, why Callahan had decided to up and
leave so soon after joining the bureau.

Maybe it was time to put in his papers. It would go a long way toward
peace in his house if he booked a vacation up to Montreal to see his
daughter and grandkids. Maybe schedule the trip for a Bruins road game
against the Canadians later in the year. He'd have to check the schedules.
The sooner he made the overture, the better.

His next week would be a series of debriefs. He'd be honest about
Callahan. He wouldn't badmouth or praise the kid. Rehearsing it in his
head, Billings said, *"Look, maybe he just missed the life he had as a local
cop. I know he didn't like how the people we catch get to walk away on some*

deal. *Nobody does. That might happen at the local level too, but not for mur-*
derers. Not to the degree we give killers new lives."

He'd work on it during the flight home. Maybe take some notes. The key
would be to play it cool, show no prejudice one way or the other. If Callahan badmouthed him, it would be easy enough to deflect the criticism. It
might even serve as a good excuse to retire.

"And then they could all go fuck themselves," he said as he dialed the
airline for a return flight to Boston.

■ ■ ■

Staten Island, New York

Special Agent in Charge of the New York organized crime task force,
Gregory Brennan, met with Detective Ovie Kaprowski outside an interrogation room at the 120th Precinct on Richmond Terrace on Staten Island. Brennan, a short man with gray hair and a thick mustache, had just
come from a formal function in Manhattan. He was still wearing his
tuxedo when he arrived a few minutes earlier. Kaprowski had slept most
of the day. He rubbed his face with both hands before picking up the coffee he'd set on a chair. He sipped the coffee as Brennan motioned toward
the interrogation room.

"He waiting on his lawyer?"

Kaprowski nodded.

"His daughter-in-law really lock him out of the house after the shooting?" Brennan said. "That true?"

"What I was told."

"That why he shot her?"

"He said it was self-defense. His only statement, according to the responding unit."

"She gonna live?"

"Winged her is all. Shot through the window and hit her in the shoulder."

"Anybody see him shoot?"

"They didn't see him, but when our guys showed up, he was still holding the gun. They verbally commanded him to set it on the stoop. It'd just
been fired. Shouldn't be a problem. He'll die inside."

"Attempted murder of your daughter-in-law. That's gotta be a new one.

Between that and losing his kid, might be he'll make a deal after all."

"He was definitely shaken up," Kaprowski said. "Only called me a cock-sucker twice since I'm here."

"Wait'll he hears what I'm gonna tell him now," Brennan said. He removed his tuxedo jacket and folded it over an arm.

Kaprowski pointed at Brennan's formal outfit. "Anything special?"

"Justice Department bullshit," Brennan said. "Some self-important judge's retirement. I left first chance I had."

Kaprowski finished his coffee and tossed the empty cup in a trash pail across the hallway.

Brennan put a hand on the interrogation room doorknob. "Shall we?"

Kaprowski nodded and Brennan opened the door. He followed Kaprowski inside and took one of two chairs at an oblong table. Gasper Cirelli, dressed in a navy blue t-shirt with a New York Yankees insignia on the chest, sat leaning forward with his head bowed down.

Kaprowski remained standing near the door as Brennan cleared his throat.

"The guy from New England still around?" Cirelli said. "I heard he tried to flip my son."

"Billings?" Brennan said. "He left for Boston earlier today. You want something to drink? Soda, coffee, water?"

Cirelli looked up at Brennan, narrowed his eyes a moment, and then turned to Kaprowski. "It's not like you didn't warn me," he said. "Or was it a bluff?"

"Look, Gasper, there's nothing left now," Brennan said. "No reason in the world to stand up. You're an old man. You're out. You can stay out. Why protect the people did this to your son?"

Gasper sat back in his chair and stared at both men a moment.

"Even if it was the guy you used up in New Hampshire," Kaprowski said, "the other crews put out the contract. Your kid was marked, Gasper. He wasn't going to survive this unless he made a deal. You know that. In your heart, you know it."

"Know what else I know, wiseasses?" Gasper said. "I know it was one of your people who called my son about Lou Testa?"

"Excuse me?" Brennan said.

Gasper smirked.

Brennan turned to Kaprowski. "You know what he's talking about?"

Kaprowski's brow furrowed. He turned to Brennan and shook his head.

"Somebody did," Gasper said, still smiling. "You want something from me? There it is. One a'yous called it in on Testa."

"I guess you'd like to believe that," Brennan said. "Maybe save face with the other crews."

"Blue fuckin' wall, right?" Gasper said. "Bunch of young punk cops choke some guy down, kill him in front of twenny people with video cameras, you got a DA afraid to wipe his ass without his voters tell him which hand to use, he don't indict. This other shine, the kid whacked in the middle of the street, middle of the day. How many shots? Twelve or some shit?" He waved off both Brennan and Kaprowski.

"Yeah, well, a mob boss lecture will probably get you a good laugh in a courtroom," Brennan said. "Why don't you save it?"

"Fuck you," Gasper said. "One of your people got Lou Testa whacked. And on that note, I'll wait for my attorney."

"Anything to say about shooting at your daughter-in-law?"

"Yeah, I almost forgot. Kiss my ass."

Brooklyn, New York

Two days after Gasper Cirelli was indicted for the attempted murder of his daughter-in-law, Detective Ovie Kaprowski mailed an overnight package to Concord, New Hampshire, from the Joralemon Street Post Office in Brooklyn. He had lunch, two dirty water franks from a vendor at Pier 6. He ate the franks under the shade of the vendor's umbrella. It was another humid summer day. The sky was dark, a thunderstorm likely. Kaprowski's Mets t-shirt was sweat-stained. He ate the franks quickly, downing a Yoo-Hoo immediately afterward.

Earlier in the day he learned from a retired police friend working United Nations security that video recordings along First Avenue had been pulled by the FBI's Internal Affairs Division. Kaprowski wondered if it had to do with anti-police protests that never seemed to end lately. He glanced at his Daily News and saw another nationwide protest was planned. He hated what was happening of late. A couple of out of control cops had fucked it up for everybody else, including anyone trying to get to and from work every day.

And worse of all, the loud-mouthed criminal pretending to be a reverend was still fueling the fire. Kaprowski wondered what the hell kind of deal the so-called reverend had made with the government to stay out of jail. Speculation on the street was that it had to do with taxes, something else for tax payers to swallow along with corporate bailouts.

"Who says crime don't pay?" Kaprowski said.

■ ■ ■

Baltimore, Maryland

He'd been home two days, and so far, at least on the news, his name hadn't been mentioned once. Tommy knew better than to assume the law wasn't looking for him. He couldn't contact his ex-wife or kids from fear the law had already tapped their phone lines. He'd used the online white pages to find the men named Joseph Collins. He eliminated those under thirty and over fifty years of age, leaving him with three possibilities. Making two anonymous calls to the Domino Sugar plant confirmed the one he was looking for still worked there, but that was all the information the second person he'd spoken to had provided.

Tommy spent two afternoons visiting a few of the bars off East Fort Avenue and learned that Friday was payday for shift workers inside the plant, and that many of the Dominoes' workers stopped in for drinks on their way home.

"At least the single ones," a bartender told him. "Divorced or otherwise."

Tommy had hoped to run into Joe Collins, but he was careful not to ask for him by name. There was also the chance the law had already approached Sandi and that she'd mentioned how Tommy had asked her about Collins.

He'd done surveillance of his own once before while hunting a piece of work for the Philly mob. He didn't like having to seek a mark out, especially if it took time. Marks usually didn't know they were being hunted. They went about their routines without concern. It humanized them and that bothered Tommy. It had made him think more than once, "There but for the grace …"

As far as Tommy was concerned, Joe Collins was different. There was no way to humanize somebody who went after young girls. Joe Collins was a dead man, except he was still breathing.

Yesterday, at his last attempt to find out where Collins might stop for a drink on his way home, Tommy lucked out in a bar on Hull Street when he overheard someone named Sparky, a loan shark it sounded like, use Collins' name.

"And tell that dickhead Collins to see my guy before he heads home tomorrow night," Sparky had said. "I have to come here to find him again, he'll be drinking his Natty Boh through a fuckin' straw."

Tommy almost wanted to tell Sparky he needed to get in line, but unless something went wrong, Joe Collins would be a corpse before long. He had to look down into his bowl of peanuts and ignore the conversation that went on another few minutes. Tommy finished his beer, left a decent tip and headed back to Towson. There was road construction on the way. The drive took him more than half an hour before he pulled into the garage under his building and parked.

■ ■ ■

Concord, New Hampshire

Robert Callahan, after three days of intensive questioning in what amounted to a twenty hour exit interview, was finally finished with his short-lived career as special agent of the FBI. Peter Billings was under investigation for what Callahan had started to suspect, and was confirmed when he was shown a surveillance video during his exit interview, the possible instigation of a mob hit on a Cirelli crime family soldier, Louis Testa.

A security camera above an ATM outside a delicatessen along First Avenue had picked up Billings making a phone call from a pay phone a few blocks north of the mugging of a diplomat and his driver. The call to a Staten Island bar had been traced to the same phone. A call from the Staten Island bar to Frank Cirelli immediately followed the call from Manhattan to the bar. When asked where he was at the time, Callahan told them the truth: "You looked into Pete, you looked into me. You already know. On the phone with my wife."

Callahan didn't know if it would be enough to implicate Billings, but he was glad to be out of the mess it might become.

Home alone while his wife was at work, Callahan spent the afternoon searching for a new job on the Internet. His wife taught at a local grammar school and was hopeful he'd return to school for a graduate degree in education, but Callahan wasn't sure it's what he wanted to do. He'd been mostly happy with the Concord police department, and had only applied to the FBI because he thought the job would be more adventurous. What it had quickly become was something Callahan detested, a lot of sitting around and waiting for criminals to cut deals. He was quick to realize that police work was more effective and fulfilling at a local level, and he already missed the job he'd left to join the FBI.

He spent some time playing with their dog, Rigoletto, before feeling sleepy at the computer. He decided to take a nap on the couch. The Bi-chon-Frise insisted on company and Callahan had to place the dog on his chest before he could nap. He felt himself drift off when the dog moved close enough to the back of the couch so it was wedged against his body and couldn't fall. Callahan slept deep until his wife woke him when she returned from work a few minutes before four o'clock.

Mary Callahan carried a package along with the mail into the living room and said, "You know an O. Kaprowski?"

Callahan was still groggy from his nap. "Who?"

"O. Kaprowski in New York. It's a package. Something soft."

"Oh, yeah, one of the cops I told you about. The one tried to get me to watch hockey. He was okay."

"Well, he sent you something."

"What?"

She set the package on his lap. "Open it," she said as she went through the rest of their mail.

Callahan used a pocket knife to slit open one end of the package, then tore the rest with his hands. Inside the package was a hockey jersey wrapped in plastic.

"What is it?" Mary asked.

Callahan removed the jersey from the plastic and held it up.

"I like it," she said. "That a real player?"

Callahan nodded. "Was on the Rangers apparently. Billings gave me shit about my name, too. I guess this was the guy he was talking about."

"Does it fit? Try it on."

Callahan stood up from the couch and held the jersey against his chest. "It'll be tight," he said.

"Then stay in shape or I'll wear it," Mary said. "What's the C for on the front?"

"Captain, I guess."

"Captain Callahan. I love it. Maybe it's an omen."

"To stay a cop?"

"Silly boy. To play hockey."

Callahan smiled, then grabbed his wife, kissed and hugged her.

Baltimore, Maryland

Joe Collins finished his shift at the Domino Sugar plant, paid the waterfront loan shark the thirty dollars in interest he owed on a thousand dollar street loan, then forked over another fifty-five dollars on a bet he'd lost with his bookie. He headed to the bar on Hull Street afterward with whatever was left of his unofficially garnished paycheck.

It was still slow at the bar when Collins sat at the hook and ordered a National Bohemian on tap. The bartender served the beer on top of a worn Budweiser coaster and asked if Collins had seen Sparky.

"I saw his muscle," Collins said. "Couldn't miss him, he was waiting for me when my shift ended. Pay day, those guys don't miss."

The bartender asked about Sparky again.

"I just says, didn't I?" Collins said, annoyed now. "I give him the fifty-five I owe, the fuckin' Erioles cost me. I bet the birds to win, they lose. I bet them to lose, they win. Cocksuckers."

"Oh, okay," the bartender said. "It's just he was here lookin' for you yesterday. Said to remind you to see him if I saw you first."

"Hey, Gus," Collins said. "Not that I don't mind your conversation, but you think I can get some peanuts here?"

Gus was a big man with a scruffy face. He frowned at Collins as he poured a pint of National Bohemian from the tap mid-bar.

Collins looked around the bar. "Where's your sidekick?"

"Bathroom."

"Which one?"

Gus set a bowl of peanuts in front of Collins, then leaned in and whispered. "You should watch yourself with that shit, my friend. She don't like you as it is."

"Fuck her."

"You wish."

"Yeah, right. I cut it off first."

A stocky woman in her early thirties wearing a low-cut Ravens shimmel shirt stepped out of the women's room. A long scar ran across the width of her forehead. She stepped behind the bar, saw Collins and said, "You're looking spry today."

"Fuck you, too," Collins said.

The woman smiled before making a half turn, pointing at an Eagles calendar on the wall and calling to Gus. "That a twenty-fourteen calendar?"

"Don't start," Gus said.

"I already seen the guy," Collins said. "You get a percentage or something?"

"Sparky's a good tipper, Joe," the woman said. "Not a cheap fuck like yourself. He asks me do a favor, I don't mind it, especially it has to do with you pryin' open your wallet."

Collins flipped her the bird.

The woman chuckled, grabbed a bar rag and wiped at the bar top on her end of the bar.

Gus asked Collins if he wanted to order something to eat.

"Your peanuts," Collins said. He removed a five dollar bill from his wallet and set it alongside his beer.

"You ever intend to knock down some of the principle?" Gus said as he took the five dollar bill and made change. "You're payin' that guy forever."

"Eventually," Collins said. "But a man's gotta eat. Got anything for me?"

Gus shrugged his thick shoulders, dropped two singles on the bar. "Not until the regular season. You'll have your tickets to move in the factory, but unless you're willing to travel, those'll only cover what you're gonna play yourself."

"Need a car to travel."

"Not to move tickets, Joe. You can hop a bus like the high school kids. You're just lazy is all."

Collins downed his first pint and pointed at his empty glass. "Yeah, maybe you're right."

Gus refilled the pint. "Anything else?"

"Some young snatch, you got it."

"You're a real asshole," Gus said.

Collins grabbed his beer and drank deep again. He set the glass down hard, tucked his chin against his chest and belched.

"'Scuse," he said. When he looked up, Gus was pouring a man wearing an Orioles cap two seats to Collins' left a shot of vodka.

"Something to eat?" Gus asked the man wearing the Orioles cap.

"No thanks." the man said.

"You new? At the factory, I mean."

"No such luck."

"Sorry to hear it."

"I tried, but they weren't interested. They says to me, they says, 'You got a record and we already employ our quota of ex-cons.'"

"That they do," Gus said. "This today, your interview?"

"Couple hours ago, yeah. I tried knocking onna few more doors before I gave up and stopped in here. You don't have anything, I suppose?"

"Sorry, no," Gus said. "But, hey, next one's on me."

The man in the Orioles cap raised his shot glass and said, "Appreciated." He toasted the bartender and downed his shot.

The bartender poured another and knocked on the top of the bar.

"I do have some cell phones I'm looking to hawk. Burners. All prepaid. Good deal you know anybody interested," the guy said.

"How much time on them?" Gus said.

"Depends. Half hour to forty-five minutes. Disposables once they're used up."

"How much?" Collins asked. He'd been listening to their conversation.

"Also depends. Interested? If you can move enough, I can go real low."

"How much is that?"

The man downed his vodka, pushed the change from his prior drinks across the bar. "Thanks, buddy," he said, then looked at Collins and pointed to the door. "I'm around the corner, up the block, that little parking lot they have there. I'll be in my car."

"Give me a few minutes," Collins said.

"Sure," the man said. "Take your time."

Collins waited until the man left the bar before finishing his beer. He slid off the stool, pulled his wallet back out, plucked two single dollar bills from it, and dropped them on the bar.

"Wow, a whole dollar tip," Gus said.

"Better than nothing," Collins said.

■　■　■

It was hard not to gut the son-of-a-bitch in the bar when he talked about young snatch, but Tommy had managed to restrain himself. He'd been staring, for one thing, except the pervert was too wrapped up in his own bullshit to notice. Tommy was grateful when the bartender called Collins an asshole and changed the subject by asking Tommy if he wanted something to eat.

As soon as he heard Collins was paying off a street loan, Tommy knew just what to do—dangle the chance to make a few bucks in front of the pervert's nose. He brought up the burner cellphones and Collins couldn't resist.

He retreated to his car parked in a lot on Hull Street between East Clement and Beason Streets. He let down the windows in the Toyota and enjoyed the breeze. The heat wave had finally ended, although it was still warm enough for a t-shirt. Tommy looked up and saw the sky was a clear blue, no clouds in sight. A perfect day to take the twins to Six Flags, watch them giggle with delight, what he missed most, their faces when they were laughing.

Last year he'd taken them down to Disney World in Orlando and spoiled them at every opportunity. Disney World, Epcot Center, Universal Studios, and then two more days down in Miami; one at Miami Seaquarium and the other relaxing on the beach, although the twins never gave him much of a chance to relax. He could barely take his eyes off them while they splashed each other at the tip of the ocean.

Thinking about them now, Tommy felt the raw emotion of ruining his relationship with them, ruining any real chance to keep his family together by getting himself arrested for trying a bank job with a bunch of morons. It had been the biggest mistake of his life until he'd started to kill for money.

He thought about Alysha and how he'd lied to her face so many times he couldn't keep count. She'd begged him for the truth, but he couldn't admit what he'd become, what he was.

And when he killed Joe Collins all his lies would be exposed. She'd know her father was a killer, and then she'd hate him.

Tommy choked down his emotions and glanced at his watch. Five minutes had passed since he left the bar. If Collins didn't show, Tommy would have to go looking for him, maybe knock on his apartment door and shoot him there.

He reached down and touched the butt of the Glock under his seat. He'd originally planned to let Collins know what it was about, tell him before he shot him in the face, then leave him for dead in the parking lot. He'd

drive out of the lot and be on his way. He could be on I-95 in just a few
minutes, North Carolina in under 5 hours. He planned to ditch the Toyota there and buy a used car for cash with one of his three remaining phony
identifications. He'd worry about the rest of his trip towards Mexico
once he put some distance from Baltimore behind him.

Then he could start his life over.

A commotion across the street drew Tommy's attention. A dozen or so
young girls in green, gray and white checkered Catholic school uniforms
were passing the parking lot. Tommy thought he spotted his twins and sat
up.

"What the hell?" he said.

The twins attended a Catholic school on the other side of the bay and
here they were with an entire class, it looked like, and without supervision.
He was about to get out of the car when he realized they weren't his girls.
He was further relieved when he saw there were two adult women shep-
herding the last of the girls forward.

Some kind of class trip, Tommy figured. Maybe down to the amusement
center closer to the water on Hull Street.

He was smiling at the thought when he spotted Joe Collins crossing Hull
Street toward the parking lot. The smile erased, Tommy reached for the
Glock again, saw the last of the young girls leaving his field of vision be-
hind Collins, and he released his hold on the gun.

"So, watcha' got for me?" Collins said, a big dopey smile on his face.

Tommy said nothing, just stared at Collins.

Collins' brow furrowed. "What?" he said. "You got somethin' to hawk
or not?"

Tommy continued staring.

"Hey, anybody home?" Collins said.

Tommy slowly smiled as he made a gun out of his hand, brought his
thumb down, and then winked. "Consider this your lucky day," he said.

"What the fuck?" Collins said.

Tommy backed out of the space, then pulled out of the lot and turned
right onto Hull Street. He glanced at Collins in his rearview mirror and
saw the asshole was giving him the finger.

"Yeah, right," Tommy said.

He beeped his horn a few times and waved as he passed the group of
young girls huddling together as they waited for the light on the corner of
East Clement Street. A few of the girls waved back. He let them cross and

had to wait for another light change before he turned left onto East Clement Street. A few more turns and he'd be on I-95 heading south. And if there was any luck left in his till, he'd make it to Mexico.

Other Charlie Stella books you may enjoy...

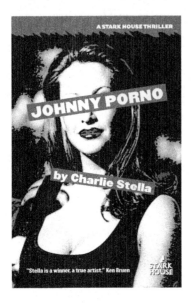

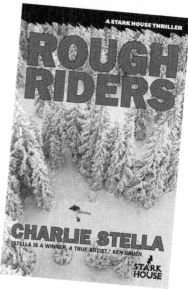

JOHNNY PORNO
978-1-933586-29-8 $15.95
"A delight." – Wes Lukowsky, *Booklist*
"Wonderfully fresh and alive."
– Craig McDonald, author of *Head Games*
"He's a true master." – Dow Mossman,
author of *The Stones of Summer*

EDDIE'S WORLD
978-1-933586-76-2 $9.99
"A sure-footed debut from a writer with a spare, no-
nonsense prose style who can make you like
characters you think you shouldn't." – *Kirkus Reviews*

ROUGH RIDERS
978-1-933586-39-7 $15.95
The sequel to Stella's first novel, *Eddie's World*.
"The dialog flows so smooth you'd swear you
were over hearing someone's conversation."
– Brian Lindenmuth, *Spinetingler Magazine*

Stark House Press, 1315 H Street, Eureka, CA 95501
707-498-3135 www.StarkHousePress.com

Retail customers: freight-free, payment accepted by check or paypal via website. Wholesale: 40%, freight-free on
10 mixed copies or more, returns accepted. All books available direct from publisher or Baker & Taylor Books.

CPSIA information can be obtained
at www.ICGtesting.com
Printed in the USA
LVOW04s1447250516

489934LV00021B/732/P